Gonna Stick my Sword in the Golden Sand
A Vietnam soldier's story

RW Holmen

Golden Sand was previously published by the author under the title *Prowl*, which has now been withdrawn from publication. *Golden Sand* includes modified material from the earlier book as well as new content. Individual chapters of this book are also available as eBooks.

Cover design by SelfPubBookCovers.com/ktarrier.

****

i

Table of Contents

Epigraph

Gonna stick my sword in the golden sand;
Down By the riverside
Down by the riverside
Down by the riverside
Gonna stick my sword in the golden sand
Down by the riverside
Gonna study war no more.

I ain't gonna study war no more,
I ain't gonna study war no more,
Study war no more.
I ain't gonna study war no more,
I ain't gonna study war no more,
Study war no more.

From *Down by the Riverside,* a traditional gospel song.

Eleven Bravo

"Now therefore proclaim this in the hearing of the troops, 'Whoever is fearful and trembling, let him return home.' Then the LORD said to Gideon, "The troops are still too many; take them down to the water and I will sift them out for you there. When I say, 'This one shall go with you,' he shall go with you; and when I say, 'This one shall not go with you,' he shall not go."

Judges 7:3-4 (excerpt)

"If'n one of them coral snakes bites you, here's the proper military procedure," droned the drill sergeant. Smokey hat tilted forward over dark glasses, uniform tight and full of starch, the tall and lean instructor stalked the stage of the outdoor amphitheater with a manner that said this was his domain.

In May of 1969, hot winds whistled through the tall pines of Tiger Village in Fort Polk, Louisiana, the training center for Vietnam-bound infantrymen. The poor bastards called this place Fort Puke, the armpit of America.

Who knew the army had a sense of humor? The joke was on us. The irony slapped you in the face on that day near the end of basic training when they posted the lists for advanced training assignments. The screw-ups in basic training--the swinging dicks

1

who couldn't hang on to the monkey bars outside the mess hall, who puked during forced marches, and who shot holes in the sky during rifle training--found themselves on this list or that one, but not on the list for 11B: the infantry, the basic foot soldiers of armies ancient and modern. Grunts. Straight legs. Ground pounders.

"... You can also use this procedure for the cobras of Vietnam, if'n one of them crawls into yer bunker when yer sleeping," the sergeant continued.

The pine slab benches sagged with fools like me, baking in the sun. Our reward for running fast and shooting straight was to be placed on *the* list. Eleven fucking bravo. While the other lists learned their specialty training here and there in comfortable camps around the country, the Eleven Bravos were sweltering in the Louisiana humidity and learning how to treat snake bite.

"Spread yer legs to a comfortable military stance ...''

Normally, we had a hard time keeping our eyes open during training sessions, and you didn't want to be caught *checking your eyelids for pinholes*, or the sergeants would poke you in the ribs. Not today. Not when the drill instructor told tales of the rattlers, water moccasins, black-widow spiders, and small but deadly red-yellow-black banded coral snakes that crawled the hill country of northwest Louisiana ... and the cobras of Vietnam. Today, we had no trouble staying awake.

"... Put yer hands on yer knees ..."

Wouldn't it be the shits to get snake bit before shipping out for the Nam? Course, if you're gonna catch a bullet anyway.

".... Bend down at the waist as far as you can ..."

The drill instructor removed his Smokey hat and wiped the sweat from his shaved head, glancing up at the merciless sun. Next, he removed his wire-rimmed dark glasses and wiped them clean as he scanned the peach-fuzz faces of the innocents. Then, he offered his wisdom, his enlightenment, his sage advice, probably like he did every day to countless Eleven Bravos who passed through his outdoor classroom on their way to on-the-job training in the Nam.

"... and kiss yer sweet ass goodbye."

****

We landed in Alaska. Even in the land of the midnight sun, it was pitch black when the jet set down on some God-forsaken spit of land somewhere out in the Aleutians, and we didn't see much from the inside of the plane. I suppose we could have seen Siberia if it had been daytime. The Soviets were the smart ones. They sent their AK-47s and their anti-aircraft batteries, but they let Charlie do their fighting.

3

We stayed on the ground just long enough for a crew change and refueling, and then we roared off into the dark night ... next stop, Cam Ranh Bay. I had been surprised when we boarded a commercial jetliner back at Fort Lewis, Washington, rather than a military plane, and I wondered if they would be passing out weapons before touching down in Vietnam--I mean it was wartime and all and who knew where Charlie might be hiding? The flight attendants didn't seem too concerned but not real friendly either, and they didn't serve drinks.

There were others on the plane that I knew: three black guys from Fort Polk who had completed Eleven Bravo training with me a month earlier. When my thirty-day leave was up and I had arrived at Fort Lewis to be processed for Vietnam, I spied their familiar faces, even if a bit unfriendly, and I had sidled up next to them in formation with all the others headed for the Nam. I surprised them. There really wasn't a race problem back at Fort Polk, but not a lot of mixing either. There was a bit of a brew stirring when some black guys started letting the other blacks into the chow line ahead of the whites, but then a sergeant laid down the law.

"Charlie won't care what color you are when he lines you up in his gun sights. You dickheads will be in a heap of shit anyway, and you better figure out now that you're all on the same side."

I don't think one of those guys had ever hung out with a white guy before because he wasn't quite sure about it, and it puzzled him

4

that the other two were congenial toward me during our short stay in Fort Lewis. Crunch time came when the four of us were drinking beers in a bar. I bought a round. The first guy bought a round. The second guy bought a round. When it came the third guy's turn, his face said, "what the fuck," and he bought the round.

Somebody once said there were no atheists in foxholes ... and no racists, either.

It took the army a couple days of processing before they had loaded us on that commercial jetliner out of Fort Lewis, and I palled around quite a bit with one of the black guys who was from Atlanta. We took pictures together in one of those instant photo places, and I mailed them home to my family. In fact, the two of us ended up in the same grunt company, until he got shot, but I'm getting ahead of myself.

****

There were no Charlies in Cam Ranh Bay after all, but plenty of sorry asses like me, spending the first day of three hundred sixty five: July 17, 1969. Mounds of white sand dunes surrounded low-lying gray buildings with tin roofs held down with sand bags. And potable water and non-potable water, but I could never remember which one was for drinking. In Fort Lewis, the army spent a couple of days processing me into Vietnam, and now that I was here, the army spent a few more days of processing, but that was fine with me. Standing in line was better than getting shot at.

A new patch on my fatigues said I was a PFC, private first class, just like all who had completed the Eleven Bravo training at Fort Polk, but then I got promoted for a few hours by somebody who needed a drinking buddy. We had been standing in a line together. The silver bar on his collar said he was a first lieutenant, and he invited me to have a drink with him at the officer's club; when he offered me his jacket with silver bars, I thought ... what the hell? Turns out the officer's club was air conditioned, and the two first lieutenants spent the afternoon drinking scotch whiskey while a Filipino woman belted out sultry jazz. I drank mine straight because I was worried about potable or non-potable water.

After Cam Ranh Bay finished its processing, they decided to send me and my buddy to the 4th Infantry Division up in the central highlands. Next stop, Camp Enari outside Pleiku. More processing. And rain. And mud. It was the midsummer monsoon of July 1969. In many places, plank sidewalks kept you out of the slimy red clay that caked your combat boots. When it stopped raining for a while, they loaded us into trucks called deuce-and-a-halfs and took us outside the perimeter for M-16 rifle training, part of the in-country welcoming festivities. There was a gully there, a drainage ditch or something, and I pictured a horde of Charlies lurking in the tall grass. I was an Eleven Bravo, and I already knew how to use an M-

16, but the clerk-typists--Remington Raiders who were sent to shoot for the one and only time in their whole damned tour of duty-- needed protection, I figured, so I kept a close eye out for Charlie, but the only real danger was if one of the desk jockeys shot himself in the foot, or worse.

More processing. We drank beer, we spent one day at the steam bath, and of course, there was the PX with a TV and an ice milk dispenser, except it was never cold enough to cool the mixture beyond a runny, slurpy mess that spilled over the top of the soggy cones. There were great bargains on electronics, but what would I do with a goddamned reel-to-reel tape deck out in the boonies? We started planning for when we'd get our first combat pay, military payment script they called it.

It was then my buddy said, "Let's go lurp. They don't ask you, you got to volunteer."

I didn't know what he was talking about. He said that lurp meant LRRP--long range reconnaissance patrol.

"LRRPs do scout work," he said.

"Who wants to be a fucking scout?" I said.

"Well, that's the bad part, but the good part is that lurps live in real barracks when they're not scouting. Half the time scouting but half the time jerking off here in the base camp. We could get us a stereo and a fridge ..."

7

"How many on a LRRP team?" I asked.

"Four or five, I guess."

"Piss on that," I said. "You gotta be crazy to go out and tromp around Charlie's jungle with just a handful of buddies to cover your ass."

He went to look some more at the stereos, and I went to get some soft, real soft, ice cream.

It was July 21 or 22, 1969, and I thought of the sky-blue waters of the ten thousand lakes of Minnesota, I wondered if Twins ballplayer Rod Carew swiped home that day, and I worried that my girl would have second thoughts if Jody was to come around (it was always Jody they warned you about--Jody's gonna get your girl, the drill sergeants teased). A small crowd gathered around the TV that hung high on a wall, and I stood at the back and watched and listened while ice milk dribbled down my wrist.

"That's one small step for man, one giant leap for mankind."

What the fuck? The TV announcer said some swinging dick was walking on the moon, and the whole world was watching. Did I give a rat's ass? What about me? Did anyone care what I was doing? Where I was? Somehow, I felt abandoned and much farther away than the man on the moon.

Humping

The dusk was repeating them in persistent whisper all around us, in a whisper that seemed to swell menacingly like the whisper of a rising wind. "The horror! The horror!

Joseph Conrad, *Heart of Darkness*

When we were finally assigned to Alpha Company, we rode in the back of a deuce-and-a-half to the secondary base camp called Camp Radcliffe near An Khe. It took the convoy two to three hours to travel the fifty odd miles. Besides us, there were two or three other fucking new guys (FNG). Alpha company was regular infantry with about eighty men led by a commanding officer--a captain--and three lieutenants in charge of the three rifle platoons, which were subdivided into three squads that included a squad leader, an M-60 machine gunner, an M-79 grenade thumper, and the rest of us were regular riflemen. Each squad had a pair of PRC-25 radios, and they assigned one to me that I stuffed into my ruck sack with the antenna sticking up and the handset clipped to the shoulder strap of my ruck. It was cool to hear the radio chatter, but that's when I made my first mistake.

Soon after we arrived, the company headed out for a major hump through the jungle and the mountains. The whole company flew in a helicopter airlift, so there must have been about twenty slicks escorted by Cobra gunships. Well, when my bird dropped us in the tall grass, I was supposed to call into headquarters and report that we were safely on the ground, but I didn't know proper radio procedures so I just said,

"Alpha Company is on the ground."

Well, they ripped me a new asshole for saying our name and especially that it was a company sized unit. You see, Charlie might have been listening and now he knew who we were and how big we were.

I think the records would say that we went humping--officially a search and destroy mission-- for twenty-three days, but let me tell you, it was a goddamned lifetime. I began as a fucking new guy, but twenty three days later I was a savvy vet promoted to Specialist 4th class (what they used to call a "corporal"); I had loaded dead comrades onto a helicopter; I had crawled over a dead enemy body to retrieve that friggin' PRC-25 radio; I had said goodbye to my friend who caught a bullet in his hand that was no big deal except it got him a ticket stateside; I had seen buddies collapse from heat exhaustion and dehydration; and at the end of it all, I volunteered to be a LRRP.

First, let me tell you about the terrain. Whether it was triple-canopy jungle or grassland, it was thick, and we would hump single-file. From the head to the tail, we stretched out around two hundred

10

meters. Imagine eighty guys strung out in a snaking line, one after the other, and you get the picture. There were times in the elephant grass that all you could do was push into it, lean against it, and when you squashed it down, you stood up, took a step forward and pushed into it again, hoping the snakes slithered away from the ruckus. Of course, that was just the guy on point, and once the grass was tamped down, the rest of us passed through easy enough, but it was a slow slog.

The three rifle platoons took turns leading the way. Within the platoons, the squads similarly rotated. Let me tell you, walking point was some scary shit, and one day the poor bastard on point took some machine gun rounds in his belly. He was still alive when he got pulled out of there and loaded onto a Medivac helicopter, and the last I heard, he made it.

One day we came to the edge of a mountain overlooking a ravine, and we were supposed to get to the other side. The captain could see no way around, so down we went into the gully. Going down was no problem, but climbing the other side was more than the captain counted on. We would grab onto a tree trunk or scrub brush to pull ourselves forward, one bush at a time, but we had a weapon in one hand and an eighty-pound rucksack on our back. Sometimes, the bush would uproot, and you would tumble back into those behind you. The guys in front would pull you up, and the guys in back would push your ass. We never made it up that day, and finally

11

darkness poured over us like somebody spilled a bottle of ink over the cliff. We stayed in place through the night, clinging to the side of the slope, wedged against a tree or rock so you could snatch a little sleep. We sure as hell were in an indefensible position, but it didn't matter because Charlie was smarter than to be walking around a mountain cliff in the dark. Whatever the reason, the fool killer wasn't around that night, which was a good thing because there sure were plenty of fools. We persisted the next morning, and the last swinging dick was up by noon, but we were so fucking tired that the captain ordered that we stop right there for the day.

Normally, the daily hump would end around 3:00 p.m. so there would be time to create a defensive perimeter, a night location or *November Lima*. Army slang was often based on the letters of the phonetic alphabet: night location=NL=*November Lima*. The small trees and brush would be cleared with machetes to create a line of fire, and the empty sandbags lashed to the bottom of our rucksacks would be filled with dirt from the holes dug with our entrenching tools. The sandbags were piled in front of the holes, and we had our bunkers. The three rifle platoons encircled the headquarters platoon. Hand activated, directional Claymore mines were arranged in a circle at the brush line with the thin electrical wires trailing back to the bunkers. Each rifle platoon would delegate four men to set up a listening post just outside the perimeter in the brush line, and we took turns with that extra hazardous duty. There would be plenty of time in the evening to break open our C rations and maybe scribble a letter home.

And that's exactly what I was doing one evening early in the hump when I thought I heard popcorn popping. Pop. Pop. Pop pop. Pop pop pop. When I realized it was rifle fire, I thought some asshole, probably one of the fucking new guys, was dicking around, but as the whole perimeter exploded in rifle fire, I knew different.

I was exhilarated. I was in mortal combat along with warriors from time immemorial. A bond stretched across the eons, and I was at one with every soldier, in every army, in every war. That was my first reaction, but such silly notions would soon evaporate.

I dropped my writing pad and dove into the bunker, and located the clackers connected to the Claymores. I detonated them all.

"Here comes a dink!" someone yelled, but I never saw him until later, when I crawled over his dead body to leave the perimeter, but I'm jumping ahead again.

Everybody was loading and reloading and pouring thousands of rounds into the brush encircling our perimeter until the order came from the captain to slow down and preserve ammo. I think we expended half our ammo just like that. Some tossed frag grenades into the brush. Charlie was too close for an artillery strike, but captain called for illumination rounds. We would hear a puff above us, and then white phosphorous burned as it slowly descended with a

13

mini-parachute, lighting up the sky. As the parachute drifted on the night breeze, shadows danced in the bushes, and we imagined Charlie was everywhere. We could hear choppers circling overhead, but they never did fire their rockets or miniguns.

The firing stopped. Had it been five minutes? An hour? More? Had time stood still?

The captain called around to take inventory. How many KIA? Four. How many wounded? Half a dozen, and one was serious. The company medic would check him out. Are all the men accounted for? Yes. Are all the PRC-25 radios accounted for? My squad leader looked at me.

"Where's your radio?"

"In my rucksack in the listening post."

You see, I was supposed to be one of the four in the listening post that evening, and I had prepared by bringing my poncho and rucksack into position, and then I returned to the perimeter to write some letters and wait until dark when the four of us would creep out. Be prepared, they say, but I had been too goddamned prepared.

My squad leader reported to the captain that one of our radios was unaccounted for, that it had been in a listening post outside the perimeter. I huddled close to the squad leader while we waited for the captain to respond, but it didn't take long.

"We need to know if Charlie has that PRC-25," the radio crackled. "If Charlie has that PRC-25, our radio security has been compromised. We need to know one way or the other."

The squad leader looked me in the eye, but I was just a fucking new guy, and he quickly looked to the others.

"I need a volunteer," he said.

Before anyone could speak, I did.

"I'll go," I said.

I was no hero, but it seemed the thing to do. I had brought it out there, and I knew where it was. No one argued with me.

"Stay low, slide on your belly," the squad leader said.

Those endless alligator crawls back at Fort Polk paid off. My left hand was empty, and my right hand grasped the pistol grip of my M-16, thumb on the safety to click to rock and roll in an instant. I hadn't gone more than eight or ten meters when I came face to face with the wide-eyed stare of a dead man, the Charlie who had been alive just moments earlier.

"Here's the dead dink," I hollered back to the others.

"Be careful he's doesn't have an unexploded grenade in his hand."

I checked, and then I wriggled my way over the top of him, keeping my eyes fixed on his blank, black eyes, as if I could see a reflection of the last thing he saw, as if I could know what he knew. I never did figure out what he was thinking to come charging in on us like that. Doped up, some said. A willing martyr, according to others. Was he just as scared as the rest of us, and when he tried to hightail it out of there, he ran the wrong way? Was he a fool or a brave hero? Only God knows, and maybe God doesn't know either.

So far so good, and I soon reached the brush line, but then I tripped a booby trap. *Christ almighty.* We had stretched a thin wire between trees about six inches off the ground, and we had affixed a white phosphorous grenade at one end that exploded about ten feet from me. This was a smaller version of the illumination flares fired by the artillery. White phosphorus burns hot and bright; I was not close enough to be burned, but the illumination lit up the night. There I was, lying in a spotlight, and I don't mind telling you that my butt muscles were clenched tight. If my nose had been pressed any tighter against mother earth, I would've been breathing worms. There wasn't a goddamned thing I could do except lay still and wait for the AK-47 round that I would never hear or for the white phosphorous to burn out, whichever came first. I'm still here so you can figure out which it was.

Darkness was now my friend, and when it settled over me, I again crabbed my way forward. I didn't have far to go, and my instincts were sound. I crawled straight to the spot, and there was my rucksack with the PRC-25 antenna jutting up from the back. I lugged

16

it behind me as I crawled back toward the others. When I got close, my squad leader scrambled out and grabbed the ruck, and I clawed my way into the bunker.

The mood that night was somber, but that doesn't really say the truth of it. My exhilaration had long since departed and depression set in as we waited for the next onslaught. No one slept, and we remained at the ready through the dark night. We had all seen too many cowboy movies and expected the Indians to attack at dawn, but they didn't; Charlie had hit and run and had hauled ass.

Who knows how many attacked us that evening? We didn't find any more bodies the next morning other than the one I told you about. Had there been other bodies dragged away? That's what our official report said, but I think that's bullshit. That's the way you snatch victory away from defeat.

But that one was still there, still staring the next morning. Maybe he's there still, or at least the skull and skeleton, and I'd like to have a visit with him one day, to ask some questions, and we never really said goodbye. Somehow I feel a kinship with him because I was there at that holy time when life became death, and I had looked deeply into his eyes, close enough to see an eyebrow twitch or an eyelid blink, but all I saw was that eternal stare. Maybe he'd like to make confession, if he was Catholic, and I could offer last rites, even if I wasn't a priest. Or maybe he was Buddhist, and I wouldn't know the words to say or the right prayers, but somehow I expect Buddha would listen anyway. I could say I was sorry and that would be the truth, but I couldn't tell him that we didn't mean him any harm, shooting him like we did, because we did mean him harm just like he meant us harm, but we could talk about that and wonder about that and talk about our families and such. At least it would nice to know his name, this man who visits me in that murky place between sleep and wake.

We were in brush too heavy for helicopters to land. Word came down that volunteers were needed to carry our dead to a landing zone (LZ) about a click away (1,000 meters). The whole company would pack up and move that way and get resupplied with ammo and such, including a few replacements for the wounded and the dead going out on the choppers. No fucking way did I want to carry those dead guys, but I got picked anyway to help with one. He was a big son-of-a-bitch, and I grabbed onto his left boot. He was wrapped in his poncho, so I didn't see his face, and I tried to imagine who he was, but I wasn't sure. I hadn't been there long enough to know everyone in the company, but I think I remember the kid from Detroit with a sad, scared, faraway look in his eyes. He was right to be scared, and so was I.

That was the longest walk of my life. I feared the next night, the next week, and the next month. As I walked that click with the dead guy's foot in my hand, I wanted to die. I was two weeks into a twelve month tour of duty. If this was the way it was going to be, I didn't think I could take it. This stiff, heavy body in my hands was the lucky one. He got it early. He was finished being scared. Maybe that's why the dead dink charged us. He didn't want to be scared any more.

When the birds lifted off, my buddy from Fort Polk and the other wounded were with them. The last I saw of him was a wave of the bandaged hand. I got a letter from him once saying he was ok back in the world, but could I buy that stereo he was looking at in the PX and send it to him?

****

That firefight happened early in the twenty-three day hump, so there's more to tell. I already mentioned the night in the ravine, and the point man who got machine gunned, but the real story of the remainder of that hump was the rain--I should say, the lack of it. Remember, it was August, and it should have been the monsoon, but it dried up, and the blue lines along with it. Streams appeared on our maps as blue lines, and it was the plan that we would refill our canteens in the blue lines. We all had canteens and water bladders hanging all over our rucksacks, and when the temperature reached 90 to 100 degrees, you can imagine how much water you needed each day, and we began to run short. A couple of times headquarters tried to resupply us by dropping canisters from helicopters, but many broke, and the water rations were barely a drip. Cans of fruit in C rations disappeared quickly. Dehydration became dangerous, and it was a good question whether we would slog ourselves out of that jungle in time before ... well, we weren't sure what could happen, but we were about to find out.

The last evening I saw one of my buddies licking something.

"Whatcha doing?" I asked.

"Eatin' jelly," he replied. "Got any?"

We went through our rucks and licked every tin of jelly we could find because there was a little moisture in there.

We made it to the last day, and we knew it was the last day, and we just needed to go up a mountain and down the other side where we would reach a highway and friendlies would be waiting for us. In fact, one squad of the friendlies would come up the backside of the mountain to hook up with us and deliver water. It fell on our squad to be on point that day, to go up the mountain first to meet up with our guides.

Goddamn I was thirsty. I was a fit person, not that there were any slackers in Alpha company, but I was able to get to the mountaintop with four or five of my buddies, while the rest of the company languished behind. Normally, our snaking string of grunts spread over a couple hundred meters would move together, but that day we got separated. Maybe it was the promise that the friendlies were bringing water that pulled the few of us up that slope, lifting one heavy boot after another up the steep incline, but we made it, and we met up with four or five grunts, but they had no idea. They had enough water for three or four but not for eighty.

I called the captain.

"Alpha six, this is two-two. Over." I had learned how to talk on the PRC-25 and how to use the appropriate code words.

"Go ahead two-two."

"Confirm rendezvous with the Delta element," I said, "but negative on the H two O."

There were silence for a moment, and then the radio crackled. "Roger. Copy. Carry on two-two. Alpha six out." Even over the radio waves, you could hear the worry in the captain's voice.

I looked at the others. Should we stay or should we wait? Our escorts settled it.

"Head straight down," their leader said, pointing with his M-16. "We've been up and down so much, you can see our trail. There's a big river in the valley and tanks are waiting on the far bank to carry you to the highway. We'll wait here until the rest of your unit makes it up the mountain."

Down we went, and it was easy like he said, especially since we all had several glugs of water from their canteens. We soon reached the valley and the river. I waded in to the knee-deep flow. I pulled out my canteen cup and filled it to the brim and drank it down. I poured the second cup over my head. I filled my canteens and waded to the shore and plopped down in the sand. The C rations included plenty to mix with the water. First, I mixed a canteen cup with Kool-Aid. Then, I heated a cup and mixed it with chocolate. Then ... hell, I don't remember all the ways I drank water, but drink I did, and I didn't care if it was potable or non-potable. Turns out it was non-potable, and those of us that drank it broke out with painful boils a week later that required lancing, but that's another story. I know I drank a couple of gallons myself over the next few hours, and I didn't piss once.

Back on the mountain, the sorry bastards were experiencing heat stroke or dehydration. I heard it all on the radio. We had seven heat casualty Medivacs by helicopter that day, dust offs they called them, and those were only the ones who passed out. Others threw away their rucksacks and their weapons. Some muckety-muck Colonel tried to take charge from his light observation helicopter circling over the troops. I think the Colonel was the battalion commander. He got on our radio push and heard all that was being said.

He broke in. "Keep the radios clear for official business. Use proper military decorum."

I heard someone key their mic. "Fuck you." And then a moment later. "I mean, fuck you, sir."

****

22

Have you ever wondered what it would be like to win the World Series? Remember those scenes where the ballplayers are shaking up champagne and spraying it around and pouring beer over their buddies' heads?

We did that.

After the hours passed and the last stragglers made it down the mountain, with the captain bringing up the rear--I give him credit for that--we all climbed atop those tanks that were waiting for us, and they carried us a few clicks to the highway. A line of deuce-and-a-halfs awaited us, and we climbed down from the tanks and into the open backs of those trucks. Now I can be plenty critical of the military and the lifers and the higher-ups and the rear-echelon warriors, but somebody had their shit together that day. In the back of every truck was a corrugated steel cattle trough--where they found six cattle troughs, I don't know--and each trough was filled to the brim with ice and cans of beer.

I don't know how long it took to drive back to Camp Radcliffe, but we were some drunk mother-fuckers by the time we got there, and our clothes and our rucks were soaked with beer. The truck driver turned up his cassette player, and Jimi Hendrix belted out Purple Haze ... *Excuse me while I kiss the sky.* We didn't know it then, but that same day Hendrix was singing the song live in a field in upstate New York at a place called Woodstock. Half way round the world, we joined in the party.

Live for today, some folks say. Yesterday's gone and tomorrow never comes. For the moment, the hump was over and life was ok again. As for tomorrow, I would take a walk down the road to brigade headquarters and volunteer for the LRRPs.

Here Comes Charlie

The greater part of the untested men appeared quiet and absorbed.
They were going to look at war, the red animal--war, the blood-
swollen god. And they were deeply engrossed in this march.

Stephen Crane, *The Red Badge of Courage*

When the door gunners tilted their M-60 machine guns to the ready, we slid our asses to the edge of the helicopter floor, feet dangling and groping for the steel runners. Gaining firm contact, we shifted our weight, including our eighty pound rucksacks, onto our feet. With my left hand grasping the edge of the chopper's door and my locked and loaded M-16 gripped tightly in my right, I glanced at the door gunner for reassurance, but the dark visor of his helmet merely reflected my own bug-eyes under a floppy bush hat, set in a face smeared black and green. Though the pilot and crew wanted to get in and out fast, the LZ slipped under the belly of the bird in slow motion. I scanned the tree line on the edge of the LZ for any telltale muzzle flashes; nothing could be worse than for a couple of Charlies to empty their AK-47 magazines into a hovering helicopter. For all the goddamned firepower on our side, the endless moment when we slowly descended into their jungle was when Charlie had us, if he was there; the best we could hope for was that he wasn't. Ready or not, Charlie, here we come.

"Jump!"

I guess five or six feet was close enough for the pilot who had a bar stool waiting for him at the club back at Camp Radcliffe. We jumped, and the slow motion chopper shifted into fast forward, departing the LZ a hell of a lot faster than it entered. We hustled across the open ground to get to the tree line and cover--unlike the time we jumped into a bog up to our thighs in goose shit and mud; it took half an hour to slog our way out of that mess, and I wouldn't be talking about it if Charlie had been watching. High above the canopy, the bird circled, waiting for our commo check before they could head for a few tall cold ones.

"Base, this is Romeo one-eight," I said into the handset of the PRC-25 radio. "Commo check. Over."

"This is base. I've got you five by five. Over."

"Roger that. See you in a few. One eight out."

With a radio link to base established, the bird disappeared; as the rapid *wump-wump* beat of her rotors gradually receded, the solitude of the jungle swallowed us. We would sit for a few minutes, back to back, rucksack to rucksack, to let our senses and our souls transition from helter-skelter to stealth. The Fort Benning Ranger-trained team leader was twenty-three; I was the twenty-one year old assistant team leader; and the two young guys were nineteen and eighteen. All we had going for us, four lurps on a Long Range

26

Reconnaissance Patrol, were our camouflage fatigues, painted faces, and the wits to disappear into the bush. *Kick the can.* Who knew that childhood variations on a theme of hide-and-seek would prepare me for recon in the jungles of Viet Nam? *Starlight, moonlight, hope to see the ghost tonight.*

The team leader whispered our coordinates into his radio. Somebody back at base stuck a red pin on a map of Gia Lai Province, Republic of Viet Nam, Southeast Asia, Earth, and The Milky Way, then returned to reading the Stars and Stripes newspaper, which provided warmed over news from home.

Earlier in the month, President Nixon had asked the "silent majority" to join him in solidarity with the Vietnam War effort, but half a million gathered in Washington to protest the war; their purpose was to "march against death." Hell, we always tried to march against death, but for us it was personal. While politicians railed about the "domino theory" and containing communism, kids my age were protesting and waving signs that suggested "make love, not war," but it wasn't up to me and my three teammates. We had no say in it, and our purpose was getting home in one piece. Like I said, for us it was personal.

In the villages and rice paddies of the lowlands, the enemy was called Viet Cong (VC=victor charlie). I suppose that's why we called the enemy soldiers "Charlies." The VC were villagers during the day and soldiers at night, but here in the mountains and the

27

jungles of the central highlands, we dealt with regulars of the North Vietnamese Army (NVA) who traveled the tributaries of the Ho Chi Minh trail that leaked across the Cambodian border forty-some miles west of Pleiku, and our assignment as lurps was to scope out their activities. We were scouts, and our mission was to gather intelligence.

We snuffed out our cigs. Time to move out. Time to find a thick brush pile to crawl into. We had landed high on a mountain ridge where the tree cover was patchy, not like the triple canopy down in the valley. The mountain spine was barely a hundred yards wide with steep declines on either side. To our left, the spine tilted slightly downward: to our right, upward. We headed up.

I always walked point, picking our way through the bush. The other three were city kids, but I had grown up in a small Midwestern town, spending plenty of time tramping around piney woods and tamarack swamps.

We snaked forward a few paces at a time in a loose string with five to ten yard gaps between us--eyes darting and ears pricked, stopping, listening, searching, sniffing--choosing each step carefully to avoid snapping a branch or kicking against a punji stick, a sharp slice of bamboo used by the NVA to booby trap pathways. Not much chance of that here, we weren't on a path, and I saw no evidence of human activity on this primeval mountain.

28

Not much brush, either. A couple of hours had passed, and we had moved a click up the ridge without finding a thicket to crawl into. Forward didn't seem promising, and we already knew there was nothing behind. Nightfall would be here soon enough, and we needed to settle in well before then. Best to move to the side, to hang on the edge just as the mountain fell away into the valley; we would have scant cover but only one direction to worry about and a handy escape route down the steep slope. We nestled into a thin patch of leafy brush and tall grass, placing our rucksacks in a row, backs to the valley. Here would be our night location, our *November Lima*, leaning against our rucks, facing up the slope, the only direction of danger; later, we would sleep side-by-side with one person awake for rotating two-hour shifts.

The team leader called in our coordinates based on dead reckoning--matching what we could see on the ground with the swirls on our charts. Did base move the red pin on the map? Did it matter? Did we really know where we were when everything looked the same? Damned sure better be right if we had to call in artillery fire or helicopter gunships.

We knew the drill; two kept lookout while the other two set out an array of Claymore mines: C-4 explosive encased in olive-drab plastic with a layer of shrapnel on the outer curve that would inflict mayhem in a controlled direction. We arranged them in a semi-circle, aimed up the slope, at the outer edge of our brush patch, 15-

20 feet in front of us, covered with leaves and grass. We also covered up the electrical wires leading back to hand-activated detonators that would lie at the ready near our feet.

With the business of war out of the way, we attended to personal comforts. We spread our poncho liners on the carpet of grass and leaves, and we cooked supper. I unsealed a packet of freeze-dried beef and rice (lurp rations were much tastier than the C-rations used by the grunt companies), and placed a canteen cup filled with water over a tiny stove consisting of an empty C-rations can with a lump of C-4 plastic explosive for fuel. Funny stuff that C-4, with the appearance and texture of pure white clay, it was highly flammable but not explosive when burned. I stirred the hot water into the beef and rice. The day before the mission, we had packed our rucksacks with all the necessities. For the planned four-day mission, we chose the best from half a dozen daily lurp rations and half a dozen C-rations and threw the rest away. Main courses came from the lurp rations but cans of fruit in a sugary syrup, crackers with peanut butter, and tins of cookies and cakes from the C-rations. The beef and rice entrée would be followed by peach sauce and pound cake for dessert.

Bellies full, we leaned back on the rucks and sucked on Camels, Winstons, or mentholated Kools. It was nearly dusk when one of the young guys slipped out the backside and disappeared over the edge with a packet of toilet paper and an entrenching tool to bury the evidence that he existed.

Crack.

A branch snapped. Goddamn it, I thought, be quiet for chrissake, but when I heard muted voices and realized the snapping branches were up the ridge, dread walloped me in the chest like falling off a swing with the wind knocked out of you.

"Get your ass back here," the team leader whispered as loud as he dared. "Here comes Charlie."

He scrambled back, and we all flopped forward, bellies on the ground, peering through the leaves and grass up the slope, butt muscles clenched tight, sure that our pounding hearts echoed over the mountainside. Without speaking, we instinctively took on different roles: I grabbed Claymore detonators in each hand; the team leader unfastened frag grenades from his belt and lined them up in front of his nose; the other two aimed their M-16s up the slope, safeties flipped to rock and roll.

The voices grew louder as Charlie drew near. At that moment, we were Greeks in the belly of a wooden horse listening to the hoots of Trojans, doughboys waiting to go over the top, GIs on a troop carrier chugging toward Normandy.

Vague shapes and shadowy faces filtered through the leaves and grass. In seconds, they would pass in front of the Claymores, unaware their lives were cradled in my hands along with the detonators. How many? Six. Eight. Maybe ten. Kill or be killed. The politicians in Washington, the generals in their air-conditioned flats, the officer corps and the lifer sergeants back at the base camp had delegated moral authority to four frightened young men, boys really, lying in the weeds. Alive or dead, our lives would forever change in the next few seconds.

We called them gooks or dinks to dehumanize them, these short, yellow-skinned men with hair black as sin whose lands we trespassed. Did their mothers feel a cold shiver pass over them at that moment? Would they leave wives and girlfriends to mourn? Fatherless babies? As the NVA filled up our gun sights, we couldn't understand their words, only their laughter.

Grasping their AK-47s by the muzzles, stocks draped loosely upon their shoulders, Charlie clearly didn't know we lay in ambush. At the slightest alarm, I would squeeze the detonators, the M-16s in my buddies' hands would spit out a full clip in a second, and the team leader would lob unpinned grenades into the melee. Some of the NVA, maybe all, would laugh no more; maybe we would be silenced too. We would all be dead or wounded, in body or soul.

I waited for the signal that never came--a cry of alarm or sudden movement. Charlie never sensed danger, and I didn't squeeze the detonators. Serendipity, I suppose, because I can't claim that I consciously decided to live and let live. Before you knew it, the young men from the north had passed by and continued down the ridge, smokin' and ajokin'. Perhaps they headed toward thatched hooches in the valley and a snout full of rice wine; little did they know they had much to celebrate. *L'chiam.* I envied the chopper crew and the squad of NVA; I had plenty to celebrate, too, and could use a couple of stiff drinks.

There was a coda yet to be heard. The rhythms of the squad that passed by had barely faded when the drumbeat up the ridge swelled again, only louder. For all the racket, it sounded like major troop movement through the bush. The squad had merely been the point, we were sure, followed by the whole fucking North Vietnamese Army. We buried our faces in the grass again, hardly daring to raise our mud-caked noses. The cacophony moved toward us like a battalion of bulldozers, but something didn't fit. The high-pitched jabbering threw us off.

What the fuck? Our heads popped up like gophers.

Monkeys. Fucking monkeys. A troop of monkeys, dozens of them, swarming through the tree tops.

****

I took the first watch as the red sun dropped behind the ridge, and pink twilight filtered through the leaves. Time for one more Kool before nightfall. A chorus of frogs serenaded as darkness seeped up from the valley and spread over the ridge. Leaning against my rucksack with the radio handset cradled next to my neck, I was glad of the coming day.

"Sit rep," crackled the voice in my ear. Every fifteen minutes, base called for a situation report.

Silently, I keyed the mic twice, the standard operating procedure that said, "Situation normal."

Cat Quiet

"Look at me!
Look at me now!" said the cat.
"With a cup and a cake
On the top of my hat!
I can hold up TWO books!
I can hold up the fish!
And a little toy ship!
And some milk on a dish!
And look!
I can hop up and down on the ball!
But that is not all!
Oh, no.
That is not all ..."

Dr. Seuss (Theodor Geisel), *The Cat in the Hat*

Survival depended upon stealth. The black and brown stripes smeared across our faces matched our tiger fatigues, and we prowled silently and slowly. Unseen and unheard, we would be hunter and not hunted.

In slow motion, I lifted my combat boot over a rotting branch and gingerly stepped to the soft ground on the opposite side. Momentarily straddling the fallen limb, I scanned the brush from left to right before dropping my gaze to the forest floor ahead to plan for my next footfall. When I was satisfied, I shifted my weight forward and lifted my trailing foot over the branch. Again and again, the methodical process was repeated as I silently crept through tall ferns, low-hanging vines, and suspended air plants of a rugged valley. Behind me in five to ten yard intervals, my three Ranger teammates mimicked my actions. Lurps on patrol.

We stalked men from the north, soldiers of the North Vietnamese Army, searching for signs of their highways or hooches, hidden from the eyes of our helicopters by triple canopy jungle. But who stalked us?

In the branches above, a noisy flock of flycatchers bobbed and weaved for bugs, while the seed-eating finches flitted here and there in the low grass and brush; the birds didn't notice us nor we them. Birdsongs and chattering squirrels said all was as it should be; silence would sound an alarm.

In an hour, we had traveled several hundred meters, but we had discovered nothing. With hand gestures, we came together in a thick patch of underbrush, and then we whispered. Which way? Stretching out again, we ascended toward higher ground, seeking a *November Lima*. Soon, the greenery of the valley gave way to brown savannah, and we moved from jungle to tall grass.

Leaving the heavy cover of the rainforest, I moved from one thicket to the next and avoided open spaces, but then we came to barren ground. The next patch was twenty to thirty meters ahead. While I paused to think it through, I saw the tall grass across the way shudder even though there was no breeze. Instinctively, I squatted and held up my hand to freeze the others, eyes fixated on the clump where I had seen movement, but the leaves of grass were now still. Too still. There were no song birds and no chattering rodents, only my pounding heart. A reddish-brown hawk with a tufted crown peered down from a perch on a dead branch of a tall thorn tree, jerking its head back and forth. I wished I could see with his eyes.

We retreated in reverse order. I now brought up the rear, walking backwards, not daring to release the grassy patch from sight. We circled around and within half an hour we were back on course, and I had nearly convinced myself that I hadn't seen anything. It was strange for me not to be on point. As the drag man, I covered our rear, and with each step forward I turned slowly and scanned 180 degrees behind us. Perhaps it was the unusual sensation of walking drag, but I felt like we were being followed even though I never saw anything to feed my foreboding.

When we reached the spine of the mountain ridge, we turned west to follow the sun. From our helicopter flyover before the mission, we knew the plateau came to a sharp point with steep declines into the valley on three sides. That tip became our goal, and our maps said we were near. When we arrived at our destination, the sun glowed orange over the mountain range that separated us from Camp Radcliffe, our base camp at An Khe. While our team leader called our coordinates into base, I made a brief inspection.

37

Perfect.

We had a vantage point over a vast swath of the valley. Any smoke curling up through the canopy from enemy campfires would be easily spotted. The grassy patches could be monitored with binoculars. Artillery batteries, helicopter gunships, even fighter jets and bombers awaited our instructions, for we were now forward observers, and we could call in death and destruction upon our dominion.

Better yet, this was a safe position. We could scramble down if it came to that, but no wandering NVA would attempt to scale the slopes. The only direction of danger was the way we had come, but who would follow the mountain spine to a dead-end drop off?

Perfect.

We bunched our Claymores, directional explosive devices activated by a hand clicker, pointing them up the spine. We seldom set out trip flares, but since the approach to our *November Lima* was so narrow, we stretched thin wire from tree to tree six inches above the ground and affixed white phosphorous grenades--illumination flares--to the ends. Even a couple of frag grenades. Any enemy traffic that happened to come our way would be funneled right into our booby traps.

Perfect.

By the time we had finished our meal of freeze-dried LRRP rations, the western sky was a palette of pinks and purples. I enjoyed a languorous last smoke, and when I snuffed out my Kool, the first pale-yellow stars had appeared.

That's when the music startled us. It came from the valley, to be sure, but where?

"Call it in! Call it in!"

Our team leader shrugged his shoulders.

"What do I say? There are dinks in the jungle? No shit."

He was right. Unless we could pinpoint the source, there was nothing we could do. Sometimes the music seemed near and then far. Sometimes to our left and then to our right. So we did nothing except to lean back against our rucks and listen to the simple stringed instrument plucked by an unseen hand. Occasionally, there would be a clang of a tinny drum or gong or other undefined percussion instrument. It was local music with a definite oriental sound, strange and dissonant to our western ears.

Then we were startled again. A plaintive female voice joined the stringed instrument, and the siren's song wafted through the heavy night air. At first I thought it must be a radio or cassette player because there could be no woman in the jungle, but she seemed real and live and here and now. And alluring. And intoxicating.

I'm not sure how long she sang, but I woke with a start and realized a chorus of croaking frogs had replaced the now silent siren, and a yellow moon had illumined the sky. My three teammates slept soundly, and I was embarrassed that I had drifted off because I had taken the first watch. Strict protocol required that one of us remain awake through the night, but it wasn't always easy to stay alert for a full two hour shift.

I put both hands on the ground and pushed myself up into a seated position, leaning against my ruck. I picked up my M-16 and checked the safety, as I always did, then laid the weapon across my thighs. Before long, I heard the familiar radio voice from the handset cradled next to my ear.

"Romeo one. Sit rep?"

A few seconds passed, and the voice came again.

"Romeo four. Sit rep?"

Every fifteen minutes, base would radio for a situation report from the teams in the field, and I'm sure half the purpose was to be a four-times-an-hour alarm clock to make sure no one had dozed off. The radio operator at base ticked off each team, and I awaited the call for Romeo one-eight. We seldom heard the response from other teams unless they had been inserted nearby. The tall radio antenna atop Hon Cong Mountain back at Camp Radcliffe was our sole contact with the world.

"Romeo one-eight, sit rep?"

I said nothing, but merely keyed the mic twice to maintain silence in our small *November Lima*, our patch in the brush and grass.

"Romeo deuce-deuce, sit rep?" The radio operator continued with his list.

Before I knew it, I heard the radio voice again.

"Romeo one-eight, sit rep?"

Had I dozed off again?

After I keyed the mic twice, I glanced at the dark sky; apparently, a cloud bank had rolled in because the moon had disappeared, and I saw no stars. I sure could use a smoke, but the burning ember would shine like a torch in this darkness. I knew some guys who would pull their poncho over their head to smoke in the night, but not on our team.

I pulled back my sleeve and checked my watch. In the blackness that smothered us like a suffocating blanket, the fluorescent dial glowed like a green beacon, and I quickly pulled the sleeve down. When base called again, I would rouse the next guy to pull watch, and I would be free to dream away. The ten to midnight shift was the best.

I thought about that music again, trying to figure who the woman was behind that beguiling voice. Was she just a cassette player? An NVA soldier? Or, was there a hooch down in the valley with a family living there that had refused to leave the jungle like the army ordered? A "free-fire zone" they called it. Since all the friendlies had been cleared out, whether they liked it or not, the only ones there had to be unfriendlies--at least according to the army--and liable to get shot. A convenient and simple morality, but I always wondered. We did have one advantage here in the boonies of the central highlands; we faced regular North Vietnamese Army--NVA-- and not the Viet Cong of the rice paddies who were your friendlies during the day but could become downright unfriendly after the sun set. Still, it nagged at me not knowing for sure. And, what about the Montagnards, the primitive mountain people who knew no life other than the jungle? How many *yards* remained on their home turf, despising both the NVA and the Americans?

I was itching to look at my watch again, to hurry it along so I could wake the next guy, then go to sleep.

And that's when I sensed it.

Movement. I don't know if I heard it; I sure as hell didn't see it, but I knew it. Somehow, our perimeter had been penetrated. Past the trip wires. What the fuck? Like flipping a switch, I was suddenly wide awake and scared shitless. Danger was practically on top of me; if I reached out into the inky blackness, I could touch it, or at least it seemed that close.

My M-16 lay across my lap, and I lifted my arms to reach for it, but when I did, the movement stopped.

I stopped.

It started.

I reached again.

It stopped.

I stopped.

The four of us lurps lay in a row, head to toe, toe to head. The other three were all on my left, toward the west. To my right, to the east, was the funnel that led into our *November Lima*, where the trip wires were set up to warn of intruders, but somehow we had been penetrated. Somehow, the movement had slipped past our booby traps. Somehow, the movement was damned near on top of me, there to my right, about to stumble into me.

It started again, circling north, moving along my legs, moving toward my feet. For the third time, I leaned forward to reach my rifle just inches from my fingertips, but as soon as I did, the movement stopped again.

Movement. What the hell is *movement?* I don't know, but it's something that moves, and I was fucking scared, but every time I tried to reach for my weapon, it stopped. *Movement* is what you reported to base when something unseen, something unknown, but something sure as hell unfriendly and after your ass was moving around and scaring the shit out of you. *Movement* was death: lurking, stalking, waiting its chance. I had movement, and somehow it had avoided our trip wires, and it was damn near in my lap, and I couldn't reach my goddamned rifle, and it was moving again.

Now it was past my feet, still moving north. I already said it was dark, so dark I couldn't see my M-16 laying across my legs, but I could feel the weapon just like I could feel the movement that I couldn't see. It was there and it was the only reality that mattered, and that's when it made a left turn and headed toward the west, beneath my feet, and in front of the only patch of sky visible in the heavens, and then I saw it, the full silhouette of a great cat.

A fucking tiger.

It stopped, right there in front of me, and turned its head toward me, and I swear I saw white fangs when it canted its head and let out the most god-awful roar that shook the trees and probably awoke all the dinks in the jungle and sure as hell roused my three buddies, who jumped around and yelled and scrambled, but it was gone.

I didn't see it leave; I don't know where it went; it was just gone.

We had heard stories of other lurps not so fortunate--of guys waking in the morning to find one missing and a bloody drag trail leading into the brush and a half-eaten body at the end of it. The tiger had scratched away our pretense and subterfuge. We fancied ourselves to be jungle cats in our tiger fatigues and painted faces, but the real feline had called us liars and exposed us. We trespassed in the tiger's lair, but our camouflage and our stealth couldn't save us, nor our perfect hiding spot, nor even the firepower a radio call away, waiting to be loosed from afar.

That's when the music started again. We heard the plucked strings, and we waited for the female voice, but it never came.

Whiskey in the Rain

Scotch and soda, mud in your eye. Baby, do I feel high, oh, me, oh, my. Do I feel high.

Kingston Trio, *Scotch and Soda*

They say you have a problem if you drink before noon. Shit, I was drinking before breakfast, before sunup, before the rest of the sorry-assed grunts in my company of ground pounders stirred from their beauty sleep.

It was the monsoon season in the central highlands, and the drizzle we had slopped around in all day and into the night had become a torrent around 2:00 or 3:00 a.m. I couldn't stay asleep in the mud as the rainwater pooled around my ass, and my poncho had become useless. I was cold, wet, and discouraged, so I got up and plopped down on an upended pail with my poncho draped over my head, and I chain-smoked Kools, as if the glowing ember would give off heat, and I warmed my insides with swigs from the quart of Johnny Walker Red that I had recently purchased at the PX.

After we had returned from our twenty-three day hump, and after we had spent a few days on "stand down" in the Camp Radcliffe base camp near An Khe, and after many of us had visited the hospital to have our boils lanced--painful skin lesions that appeared after we had chugged down water from a polluted river, and after I had tramped up to the brigade headquarters and volunteered for the LRRPs, and after we had been moved out of the barracks to this muddy cesspool outside the perimeter of the base camp, and because I only had a few more days as a straight-leg infantryman before the brigade cut the orders to transfer me to the LRRPs, I figured a little whiskey in the rain was called for, even if it was a bit early in the day.

****

Remember those old John Wayne movies where he just turned and slugged someone in a barroom in the old west, and the place exploded in a brawl, just for the hell of it?

We did that.

The Filipino bands that played at the Non-Commissioned Officer's (NCO) club in Camp Radcliffe got the juices flowing. They covered rock and roll classics, and the table seating was surrounded with standing-room-only GIs swaying to the beat of *Proud Mary*. When one of my lurp buddies left his table seat to whizz in the piss tube outside, an empty rocket canister with one end stuck in the ground, a stranger slid his ass into the empty chair. When the lurp returned to claim his seat with shouts and shoves,

47

attention switched from the sultry Filipino female lead singer to the islands of bush hats and tiger fatigues floating in the smoky haze. If lurp camo fatigues helped us to be invisible in the jungle, they had the opposite effect in a bar crowded with rowdy GIs, and it was tiger fatigues versus olive drab. What happened next was all harmless, a barroom brawl straight out of a Hollywood western that allowed us all to let off some pent up steam.

When the MPs arrived to settle things down, they unpeeled a pile of wrestlers, and they found me on the bottom with a stranger in a headlock. Sort of like John Wayne telling the piano player to keep banging on the keys, the Filipino band started rockin' and rollin' again, and by the time they closed with the classic, *We Gotta get out of this Place,* crazy-assed warrant officers who piloted the Hueys and Cobras were frolicking on tables, and I danced on the edge with my new acquaintance from the bottom of the pile.

****

Our LRRP mission was radio relay for an infantry company. The ground pounders would be inserted into a deep ravine, and we would be their ears atop the ridge. Because of the topography, their radio signals wouldn't reach their headquarters back at Camp Radcliffe, but they could reach us, and we would relay their communications to their base who would respond through us.

48

We were inserted a few hours ahead of them, and we set up our *November Lima* in a thicket alongside the steep slope that dropped into the ravine. Our team leader showed off his skills learned in Ranger training back at Fort Benning by jury-rigging an antenna array strung out in low hanging branches. By the time the stream of slicks offloading the grunts arrived, we were ready, and the first commo checks worked fine--*five by five, lima charlie (loud and clear)*--but as the slicks kept coming and going, we lost contact. We tried several pre-arranged frequencies, but there was no response from the grunts in the valley below. The slicks had stopped flying, night was falling, and still no response from the infantry company. What was even more quizzical, our radio contact with their headquarters also dropped off, and we couldn't raise anybody on that end either. When we'd flip back to our own lurp company frequency, our radios worked just fine.

The mystery continued through the night and into the next day. Finally, we asked our own headquarters to get on the landline with the grunt headquarters to see what the hell was going on. We soon heard back from base.

"Move back to your LZ. Birds will come to pick you up in an hour."

When we were aboard a slick heading home, our platoon lieutenant finally told us what was going on.

"The grunts pulled out even before they were all in, and they simply forgot about you."

No fucking shit. For a day and a half we had been trying to make contact with a goddamned grunt company that wasn't there. We were four lonely lurps on a ridge covering their ass, but they forgot about us. So fucking typical.

We were plenty pissed alright, but we were polite the next day when the grunt company commander personally visited us at Ranger headquarters to apologize. He brought two bottles of Crown Royal in velvet sleeves as a peace offering. On the bright side, since the mission was cut short, we had a few extra days to spend in the rear, and that Crown Royal helped us develop a taste for Canadian whiskey.

****

The first time I smoked a reefer was on a convoy.

Long lines of deuce-and-a-halfs hauled back and forth between An Khe and Pleiku, the two principal cities of the highlands and the location of the two sprawling base camps, Camp Radcliffe and Camp Enari. Cobra gunships escorted the convoys along the fifty mile journey, and the highway was guarded by intermittent firebases and strategically placed tanks. Though the history of Highway 19 included gory ambushes, the most famous being the rout of the French at the Mang Yang Pass in 1954, we considered traveling in the convoy to be a Sunday stroll compared to our missions in the field.

The higher-ups in the central highlands could never quite decide where they wanted their LRRP headquarters, and we were transported back and forth several times between the two base camps. On this trip, I climbed into the cab with the driver to ride shotgun. We had barely cleared the perimeter of Enari when the joints began to circle in the back of the deuce-and-a half, and the swinging dicks back there were kind enough to flip up the canvas flap that covered the rear window of the cab and pass joints to the driver and me. *What the hell.* I took some hits. Nothing. No buzz. This is no big deal, I thought.

We traveled a few more miles down the road, and I happened to notice one of the many tanks that perched on knolls guarding the highway. No, I didn't just notice it, I fixated on it as we moved by in seemingly slow motion. "Fuckinnnng Aaaa, man. Look at that fuckinnnng tank." It was the coolest thing I ever saw. Maybe I was stoned.

I wasn't really paying attention, but a light observation helicopter circled overhead. Turns out it was a fucking general who noticed the lurps in the back ends of the deuce-and-a-halfs weren't wearing steel pots. We never wore those heavy helmets in the field, relying instead on camouflaged bush hats, so why the hell did we need to wear steel pots while enjoying a leisurely drive through the countryside? The general saw it differently, and he landed his helicopter up ahead to stop the convoy and have a few words with the butter-bar second lieutenant in charge of the lurp contingent. That the lurps in the back of the trucks had flipped the general off might have had something to do with it. You never saw a man stand straighter or stiffer than that poor second looey while the general reamed him out. When Colonel Klink was through with Sergeant Schultz, and Hogan's Heroes were told to put helmets on our heads, we had a hard time stifling our snickers, especially since we were all stoned.

Yup, there were drugs in Vietnam, and you tended to be either a "juicer" or a "head," but the lines were fuzzy. Ha, that's a play on words. Of course, I'm talking about our time spent in the rear, and we were always stone-cold sober when we were in the bush. I drank my share of bourbon and beer, but I also disappeared into the tall grass outside the barracks a time or two when a joint was passed around.

Then there was Hon Kong Mountain, a rocky peak inside the perimeter of Camp Radcliffe that towered over the An Khe plateau, a landmark visible from miles around. Radar installations and an array of radio towers perched atop the lofty crags, and Hon Kong Mountain was home to a clique of technicians. The cloistered community atop the mountain had plenty of spare time to get in trouble, and they did. There were a few times that a couple of us either walked up the dusty road that twisted to the top or hitched a ride because we knew you could get stoned up there.

One time, a dozen or so swinging dicks gathered in one main hooch, and there were thick joints for everyone, plus one, that got passed around so you could barely keep up. Afterwards, the owner of the hooch invited me up a rickety ladder onto his flat roof of corrugated tin. We slowly twisted in a circle, surveying the landscape and the hazy horizon in each direction. The mountain ranges, the jungles, and the overgrown grasslands seemed damned peaceful from this vantage. After we took it all in, a shit-eating grin spread across my host's face, and he repeated his favorite line that he uttered on all such occasions.

"You're now the highest person in all of Vietnam."

Chasing After Wind

No one has power over the wind to restrain the wind, or power over the day of death; there is no discharge from the battle ... all is vanity and a chasing after wind.

Ecclesiastes 8:8 & 1:14

The weather vane atop the LRRP headquarters building caught my eye. I hadn't noticed it before that morning, and it took a couple of glances to figure out that the ornament was a joker, like you would see in a deck of cards, and the joker's wand pointed toward the wind. Roll call came at 7:00 am, and while I stood in a casual formation with the rest of the 3rd platoon, I watched that joker dance and spin. First the wand pointed west. Then the damn thing spun around, and it pointed north. I kept one eye on that spinning joker while they passed out the malaria pills. I tossed both down without water, a little one and a tablet the size of a horse pill. A dust devil kicked up sand that stung my face, and when I wiped my eyes, the joker now pointed east.

After the morning formation, we strolled across the company grounds in a loose line to police the area for any trash that had blown in since the day before, and there seemed to be plenty that morning.

When we finished, we hurried toward the mess hall and breakfast, and now the joker's wand pointed south. The wind blew where it would, and I was still puzzling over that joker when the mess crew filled my tray with scrambled eggs and bacon, but with the first sips of steaming black coffee, my mind moved on.

I spent the morning shooting the shit. Our four-man lurp team had been back at base for a couple of days, and we had a couple more before our next mission. Lurps faced danger in the field, but you couldn't complain about our down time at base camp. The morning roll call was about the only official business, and then you could do as you damn well pleased for the rest of the day.

Right after lunch, I took a seat in a poker game. Some days, luck is against you, and you'd be better off just walking away, but how do you know when that is? What if your luck is about to turn? I'd been playing about an hour and my chips were slowly dwindling, but this hand looked damn good, and I figured this was my chance to get even.

The game was five card stud, and my hole card was the ace of spades. The dealer dealt the ace of clubs for my up card giving me a pair of bullets.

"High card bets," the dealer said, looking at me.

House rules for the running poker game in our barracks allowed two dollar limits and three raises per round. If I'd bet two bucks, I probably would have won the pot right there, but it needed to grow a bit first.

"Open for fifty cents," I said, and I flipped in a red chip.

"Fold."

"Fold."

The two guys to my left dropped out.

"Call," the next guy flipped in a red chip. His up card was the six of diamonds.

"Raise," said an E-6, and he tossed in a red chip for the original bet and two blue chips for his raise.

I didn't know the raiser very well because he hadn't been around that long. He was a staff sergeant, E-6, and that normally meant lifer, but he was fresh from Ranger school at Fort Benning, and he was pulling LRRP missions like the rest of us. Hell, he was probably younger than me, and I was only twenty-one. Judging by the peach fuzz on his cheeks, he hadn't shaved in a couple of days, but he could probably manage a few more without any problems. He wore fatigue pants bloused over combat boots, but no shirt covered his pale chest or the dog tags that dangled from his neck. He had been winning that day, but it seemed to me that he overplayed his cards, and the jaunty tilt of his bush hat said he wasn't afraid to gamble. The deuce of spades that was his up card wasn't very impressive.

Why'd he raise? Must have a pair of deuces, but that wouldn't beat my aces.

"I'm out," the next guy around the table said, and the bet moved to the dealer.

"I fold," the dealer said as he flipped over his up card, the deuce of diamonds, which was a key card if my hunch was right that the E-6 had a pair of deuces.

It was back to me, and I thought about re-raising, but I slow played that sucker and just called, and the six of diamonds called also. Three of us remained in the hand.

"Eight, no help," the dealer said as he dealt the eight of clubs to go with my face-up ace. He offered running commentary as he dealt the next cards.

"Ten, no help."

"Nine, no help," the dealer said as he turned over the nine of hearts to go with the raiser's black deuce.

"Your ace is still high card. Ace bets," the dealer said to me.

"Two bucks," I said, throwing in a pair of blue chips. If they both folded now, that would be alright.

"I'm out," the six of diamonds said as he turned over his up cards.

I was surprised when the E-6 raised me again. With a deuce and a nine off suit showing, he had diddly, but he raised anyway.

"Make it four," he said.

His ass was grass.

"Make it six," I said.

"Might as well make it eight."

He made the last raise of the round.

On Fourth Street, another face-up card, I drew the nine of diamonds, and he drew a jack, but it didn't matter; he kept raising my raises as if he had a joker in the hole, but we didn't play with jokers. It was again an eight dollar round.

The last card was dealt down, and I drew the eight of spades giving me two pair, aces over eights, the so-called dead man's hand. They say that was the hand Wild Bill Hickok was holding in Deadwood when he got shot in the back, but I was happy to draw that eight. The only way the E-6 could beat me would be to suck out, and that's just what he did. His luck continued to run hot and mine cold.

Just like I suspected, he had been raising all along on a fucking pair of deuces! A third deuce had been face up in the dealer's hand so there was only one deuce left in the deck. Only the case deuce could win the hand for him, but that's what he drew. The goddamned deuce of clubs. His trip deuces beat my two pair.

I lost about fifty bucks in a little over an hour, most of it on that hand, and I walked away from the game. It wasn't my day, but it sure as hell was his. *Christ almighty*, a pair of fucking deuces.

I had been sitting on a foot locker with my back against the wall, and the E-6 was straight across from me, with his back to the aisle, and the guys had to stand up to let me out. The barracks wall behind me was plastered with playing cards; every time a new deck was opened, the jokers were hammered onto that wall. As I stood up, one of the figures caught my eye. It was the same goddamned joker of the weather vane atop headquarters; up close I could see the hideous laugh pasted on the sprite's face. It seemed like that son-of-a-bitch pointed his wand straight at me.

"I need some beers," I said.

The card game was in the center of the barracks between a pair of bunks that butted up against the wall. It was an extra wide space where the running poker game went on for lurps spending time in the rear between missions. Players would come and go, but the game rolled on.

I shuffled back to my own AO, that's what we called our "area of operations," that I shared with a couple of buddies. Three of us had arranged our bunks to create a room, two bunks perpendicular to

59

the wall and one parallel to it along the outside of the AO. The mosquito netting that draped down over the bunks provided walls and a little privacy. Courtesy of the PX, we boasted a mini-fridge, a Panasonic cassette player, and a couple of beach chairs, all lined up against the barracks wall. I cracked open a cold one, and the suds ran down my hand and dripped on the cement. One of the guys was there reading a book, but he set it down when I returned. He wasn't a card player, so he didn't understand when I tried to explain the crap that had just happened to me.

For the next hour or so, we listened to the Beatles latest album release called *Abbey Road* on the Panasonic and drank beer.

Later in the afternoon, it sounded like a little ruckus or something was going on with the poker game, and I poked my head out of the AO to check it out. I heard buzz talk among the ever-present kibitzers that one of the teams in the field was in contact with the enemy.

Contact. Lurps dreaded that word. *Contact.* It meant that your primary defenses of stealth and subterfuge had failed, and your four-man lurp team had been exposed far out in the bush amongst the hooches and the pathways of the North Vietnamese Army that traveled the mountain gulleys of the Ho Chi Minh trail. When the shooting started, you screamed into the PRC-25 radio, "Contact! Contact! Romeo one-eight in contact!" and you called for Cobra gunships with their rockets and six-thousand-round-per-minute miniguns to light up the jungle and for slicks to return to extract you, but in the meantime you exploded your Claymores, you emptied clips of M-16 rounds, and you tossed frag grenades; sometimes you crawled away into the brush, but disengaging from contact while hanging with your team and finding your way to an LZ was hairy as hell. You relied on instincts and training, and you did what you had to do to stay alive. Every contact was different and had its own rules, and the only constant was that you were scared shitless until the birds came and you were on board, flying toward base. That's when the fear subsided, leaving just the adrenaline coursing through your veins.

I returned to the poker game to hear what was going on. It sounded like the team was ok and working its way to an LZ, but a couple of enemy soldiers from the north, the NVA, had bought the farm. It wasn't unusual for one of the lurp teams in the field to be in contact, but it was a little different to hear real-time reports. There was a dark room in the headquarters building with maps wallpapered on all sides, and that's where the radio operators huddled with the commanding officer and the other higher-ups during a contact. There were landline telephones with connections to the helicopter squadrons and artillery batteries and all the firepower and support the army could muster, but the rest of the Rangers in base camp typically didn't hear reports until the team made it back.

The E-6 continued playing his cards aggressively and continued winning. Some days are like that, when luck is on your side and you played it for all it was worth because it could turn on you just like that. Most of the crowd departed for chow at the mess hall, including a couple of guys at the poker table, but others slid into their places, and the E-6 said somebody should cook him up some lurp rations, and before long boiling water was poured into freeze-dried chili con carne, and he ate it on the spot while he kept raking in more than his share of the pots. His luck hadn't turned yet, and no way would he surrender the hot seat.

The word in the mess hall was that the team was still in the shit. They hadn't been able to break contact like they thought, and they hadn't made it to the LZ yet. What was worse, it would soon be dark, and a nighttime extraction would be especially dicey. The chopper pilot depended on you to find a wide LZ so there would be no branches snatching the rotors when you guided the bird down with flashing strobe lights.

Damn, it was hot. It was always sweltering in the central highlands of Vietnam, but it seemed especially prickly that evening. Like a stalking beast holding its breath, the wind that couldn't make up its mind all day now hesitated altogether, and no breeze filtered through the screen windows of the mess hall. Tall clear glasses filled with ice and cherry Kool-Aid sweated droplets of water that looked like blood streaking down the sides. I lifted the cold surface to my forehead, and then I sucked on an ice cube. By the time I finished the macaroni and cheese and boiled hot dogs slathered in mustard, word came that the team was in a chopper and enroute to the base. Safe.

I figured maybe it was time to get back in that poker game, but all the seats were full when I got there. I put my name in, but there were a couple of swinging dicks ahead of me, so I returned to my AO. By now, it was pitch black outside, and the lights in the barracks glowed a hazy yellow in a blue cloud of cigarette smoke. I plopped down in one of the beach chairs and lit up a Kool and smoked it slow.

Loud voices announced that the team had returned from the field. I poked my head out and looked toward the poker game. One of the team was there with his bush hat and painted face streaked with white sweat trails. He had set his rucksack down on the cement floor and was talking loud and fast and gesturing with his M-16 held by the pistol grip in one hand as he was telling the others about the contact. Adrenaline was still pumping through his veins, and he was feeling the rush of combat without the fear.

A gust of wind blasted through the barracks from the open door on one end and slammed the door on the other, and I felt a chill as the breeze rushed past. Suddenly, my gut told me something wasn't right. A colored stencil on the black plastic of the forward hand guard of the M-16 pulled my eyes in. What I saw told me that the luck of the poker-playing E-6 was about to run out, and my jaw dropped open to shout a warning. The joker with the haunting grin danced on that hand guard as the lurp waved the M-16 muzzle right behind the head of the E-6. The M-16 was loaded with a full clip, and somehow I knew that the safety was switched to rock and roll, and somehow I knew that the adrenaline-intoxicated lurp from the field was about to squeeze the trigger, but my scream was drowned out by the burst of four or five rounds.

The E-6 slumped forward onto the poker table, and red, white, and blue poker chips scattered. The back of the sergeant's head was gone, and his blood splattered the jokers tacked to the far wall.

****

They called incidents like that "friendly fire," and the army probably awarded the dead sergeant a medal as if that would make his death valiant and meaningful. He was dead-dead, but the poor son-of-a-bitch that shot him was alive-dead, and he would live his death tomorrow and next week and every day.

For several hours, the barracks swelled with the comings and goings of higher-ups, medics, MPs, and who knows who, but I cleared out. I grabbed my poncho, poncho liner, a beach chair, a carton of Kools, a jug of Kentucky whiskey, and a transistor radio. I intended to spend the night under the stars in the patch of tall grass outside the barracks, but there were no stars, only dull gray clouds that scudded across the sky, roiled by a growling wind. I sucked on

Kools chased with slugs of bourbon and listened to the radio blaring Jim Morrison and the Doors.

Show me the way to the next whiskey bar. Oh, don't ask why. Oh, don't ask why. For if we don't find the next whiskey bar, I tell you we must die. I tell you we must die. I tell you, I tell you, I tell you we must die.

In the middle of the night, the clouds spit out a sprinkle, and I pulled my poncho over my head and slouched down in the beach chair and fell asleep. I awoke when the disc jockey played the Beatles' Abbey Road album, and the same George Harrison song I had listened to earlier in the day.

Here comes the sun, here comes the sun, and I say it's all right. It's all right.

The wind had died, and the sky glowed yellow in the east as I trudged back to the barracks for another hour of sleep before roll call.

Elijah Fire

If I am a man of God, let fire come down from heaven and consume you and your fifty.

2nd Kings 1:10

"They shot my fucking legs off!" my lurp teammate moaned as the Cobra gunship screamed by, barely clearing the treetops over our heads.

There is no sound like the chainsaw groan of the six-thousand-round-per-minute miniguns of the Cobra. With one pass over a football field, a Cobra would spray fifty-caliber rounds into every square foot, or so they said, but now the son-of-a-bitch piloting that killing machine had opened fire before waiting for our lurp team to pop smoke. Colored smoke wafting up through the treetops would be our signal, our plea, our prayer, "for Chrissake, don't shoot here!" Why had the Cobra gunship failed to follow Standard Operating Procedure?

****

We were damn-good sneaks, and usually Charlie didn't know we were sniffing around his jungle lair, but sometimes painted faces and cat quiet stealth weren't enough. If Charlie wandered too close, we would surprise him with bursts of M-16 fire plus a few Claymore mines and frag grenades mixed in, but the puny firepower of four lurps in the field couldn't sustain a serious firefight. That's when we'd call in hellfire.

Here's an example. Just a month or so earlier, our four-man lurp team had landed in a clearing slanted along the side of a mountain ridge. We jumped the last few feet, and we were lucky our legs weren't impaled on the punji sticks hidden in the tall grass. Charlie must have expected that clearing to be an LZ one day and jabbed the ground with sharpened bamboo sticks dipped in shit. A punji stick wound was a painful nuisance, prone to infection, but seldom fatal. We scrambled up to the trees arrayed in single-file vigil along the spine of the ridge, and the cooking utensils and warm ashes we stumbled upon said someone had watched us land before hightailing it out of there. Sometimes our lurp team ended up in an area devoid of Charlie, but this would not be such a mission. Charlie was close by, and we knew it. What was worse, Charlie knew trespassers had invaded his domain.

We reversed course and headed down through the tall grass toward the triple canopy jungle at the base of the ridge. When we arrived, it was too friggin' quiet. I was on point as usual, and I held up my hand for the others to halt. We raked our eyes back and forth, but we didn't spot anything lurking in the ferns and underbrush at the edge of the jungle. After momentarily hesitating, we slipped into and through the heavy foliage. As soon as we moved under the triple canopy, the vines, shrubs, and small trees disappeared, and we were in a clearing. The heavy cover prevented sunlight penetration to the floor of the rainforest and thus no underbrush. We squatted to reconnoiter. The absence of birds flitting about the under layer of the foliage above was spooky. The rainforest was normally a cacophony of birdsongs, chirping rodents, and maybe even chattering monkeys, but the silence said the jungle knew intruders were present.

My nose wrinkled and nostrils flared. Wood smoke. I turned and made an exaggerated sniffing gesture to alert the others. Then I did something stupid. I followed the scent rather than retreating, but it was our good fortune that the fool killer wasn't around that day. Creeping on that jungle floor without ground cover was like parading in your underwear down Main Street, and when a hooch appeared in front of us, we foolishly kept going. Curiosity can kill. With each step forward, we hesitated and scanned for signs of life. We paused in front of the thatched-roof hut on stilts, and inspected it without entering. Could be booby trapped. It seemed empty and so did the next one in line. In fact, we realized we were on the edge of a whole array of hooches hidden from the prying eyes of the sky by the triple canopy cover, and still we crept forward, but then a mangy dog brought us to our senses.

The patchy-haired mutt came trotting along, happy as you please, with one ear flopped back, but suddenly we were face to face, and we both stopped and stared. His ears perked up, and the hairs along his back bristled, but he didn't growl or bark. He just glared at me like he was puzzling, "who the fuck are you?"

I think that mongrel saved our lives because his beady-red gaze burned with the eyes of a thousand creatures watching us, and we suddenly realized we were emperors with no clothes. We retreated from that hidden village much more quickly than we entered, but we had nowhere to go and nightfall was fast approaching. It was too late in the day to wander in search of an ideal *November Lima*, especially since all signs said there were plenty of Charlies around, so we just plopped down in the thickest clump of undergrowth we could find, sandwiched between the tall grass of our arrival LZ and the open ground under the triple canopy. We didn't set out Claymores, and we ate a cold supper. I pulled out a Kool to light up, but my team leader grabbed it from my lips and crumpled it in his palm. Not a good time or place for a smoke. We barely whispered and dozed in snatches on the tilted ground of the mountainside.

Dawn arrived with gunfire, but it wasn't near nor was it frenzied like a firefight. It came from the direction of the hooch village a couple hundred meters away, and the firing was slow and rhythmic. Pop. Pop. Pop.

"They're shooting their livestock," our team leader speculated. "They know we're here, and they know we've found their lair," he added, "and they're preparing to haul ass."

Here's where I finally get to the point of this story. We called in hellfire. We moved up the mountainside to find a vantage point in order to become forward observers for a field artillery unit located miles away. We would be the gun sights for their howitzers, and we would blow those hooches to kingdom come. Charlie was clearing out, and it was too late to catch him, but we could destroy his hidden village, undoubtedly a way post in the labyrinth of the Ho Chi Minh highway that snaked through the gullies of the central highlands.

Our team leader targeted latitude and longitude coordinates based upon the known coordinates of our LZ. The first spotting round fell short by half a click. The team leader called in adjustments, and the second spotting round walked closer.

After the third hit the target dead on, the team leader spoke clearly into the PRC-25 handset. "Fire for effect," he said.

We hunkered down and waited for the telltale whistle of incoming high explosive rounds. Fireworks on the fourth of July are mostly flash and sizzle eye-candy; real artillery explosions were heard and felt more than seen. We wished we had plugs, and we covered our ears the best we could with our palms. With each ear-splitting detonation, the earth rumbled, and the sentinel trees along the ridge line quivered. Long before the barrage ended, I had serious doubts about the wisdom of calling down fire from on high so close to our position.

When the din finally ceased, our PRC-25 radios said that birds were in the air delivering a grunt infantry company to our location. We were advised to move to the LZ and to pop colored smoke to guide the pilots in. We quickly policed as many punji sticks from the LZ as we could. We were to depart on the first bird and let the infantry company sweep the area. We knew that all they would find would be a burned out hellhole.

Red leg artillery wasn't the only hellfire at our disposal. Here's another example from another LRRP mission.

A series of mountain ridges had been folded together like an accordion. Our *November Lima* was in a rocky outcropping perched atop the first ridge overlooking an expansive plateau to the east and the succession of ridges to the west. Separating us from the next ridge was a deep-cut gully with steep slopes on either side. We had found this perch the first day of the mission; it suited us, and we stayed there for the duration.

On the third day, the eastern sun filtered through the tree tops and warmed my sleeping face. Two of the other guys woke about the same time. The fourth had pulled the dawn watch--one guy stayed alert through the night in two hour shifts--so he had been awake for a while when the other three of us rubbed the sleep from our eyes and began to heat water in our canteen cups for instant coffee. A used can from a pack of C-rations made for a good stove fueled by a lump of combustible C-4 plastic explosive.

"I heard a loudspeaker in the gully," the dawn-watch guy said.

I lifted a sleepy eye in his direction. I was dubious. Charlie was secretive like we were, and a loudspeaker in the jungle was incongruous and seemed unlikely. Plus, this was the guy who always claimed his hearing had been damaged by loud explosions. I leaned against a boulder as I sipped hot coffee with long pulls on a Kool.

"Not just once, but several times," he claimed.

One of the other guys rolled his eyes.

It's pretty surprising how much you can hear when you're intentionally listening for something. The wind rushing through quaking leaves, dozens of unique bird calls, occasional shrieks from an unknown creature, but no goddamned loudspeaker. We listened hard for the next hour, and our doubts swelled. With each new bird call, we screwed up our faces with looks that asked, "Was that it? Was that what you heard?"

The more we doubted, the more his faith grew. Finally, he said, "I'm calling it in."

We had front row seats for the entertainment that followed. First to arrive was a fixed wing "bird dog," a small plane that circled overhead and communicated first with us to identify the target and then with the Phantom fighter jets that strafed that gully. The first jet to arrive scared the shit out of us. We didn't see it coming, and our first notice was the sonic boom that shook the trees as the jet screeched out the far end of the valley. After that, we watched closely as the Phantoms approached from the south. From our rocky perch high on the ridge, we actually looked down on the jets as they roared into the valley for a split second on their strafing runs.

For good measure, a pair of WWII vintage fighter aircraft, probably hellcats, arrived after the Phantoms departed. Each of the retired champions, still frisky and anxious to stretch their legs, made a few runs through the valley with guns blazing.

I'm sure the official records note a great victory, but I suspect we merely knocked over a bunch of trees and killed a swarm of jungle critters.

****

The Cobra gunship remained our closest ally and purveyor of wrath from the sky, so it was cruel irony when my teammate's fearful voice cried out, "They shot my fucking legs off!" How had it come to this?

Hours earlier, our four-man LRRP team had been inserted into a comfortable LZ. This was the odd mission that didn't carry us to the jungle or the mountains; instead, we were inserted onto a plain that had once been farmland but years of war had allowed the elephant grass to grow head high. The grassland was dotted with clusters of small trees, and we quickly moved from the LZ into the thickest woodlot we could find. Once inside, we set up our *November Lima* in a dense patch of low brush. We arrayed our Claymores in a 360 degree circle around us and settled in.

It was then that the whir of the Cobra rotors first sounded in the distance, faster and higher pitched than the *wump-wump* of the slick that had transported us to the bush. Surprisingly, the Cobra pilot hailed us on our push. Usually, our only radio contact was with base; artillery support, fighter jet support, or helicopter support would only occur *after* we had requested it from base, and the support group would then join us on our radio frequency.

"Romeo one-eight, this is Elijah five-oh," the Cobra said. "We're hunting in your neighborhood, and we'll be close by if you need help."

At the time, the words were comforting.

Ten minutes later, maybe fifteen, I was cutting open a tin of pears in a clear sugar sauce with my standard issue P-38 can opener. The other guys also finished their lunch, but one guy suddenly flopped to the ground and pointed. I spilled my pears when I rolled

74

over, but I couldn't see anything in the thick brush. I was surprised when he fired a single shot, and then he fired off a full sequence of single shots. The other guys flipped their M-16s to rock and roll and lit up the brush in the same direction. I still hadn't seen anything, but I grabbed the handset to my PRC-25 radio and began to shout over the crackling gunfire.

"Contact! Contact! Romeo one-eight in contact!"

While my teammates continued to lay down small-arms fire, I maintained radio contact with base, and that's when the Cobra again came on our push.

"One-eight, this is Elijah. We're thirty seconds away," said a friendly voice.

I detached a smoke grenade from my rucksack and awaited the request of the gunships to pop smoke. After receiving this Standard Operating Procedure request, I would pull the pin on the grenade and allow colored smoke to waft upward through the trees. Normal SOP would require the Cobra to report sighting of the smoke and its color--"I've got goofy grape"--which I would confirm. That process would serve to mark the spot where the gunship *shouldn't fire*.

The request to pop smoke never came. The next sound I heard was the whine of the mini-guns and the cry of my teammate, "They shot my fucking legs off!"

Without lifting my head, I gator crawled over to him, expecting to find his life ebbing away in spurts of blood.

"You dumb son-of-a-bitch," I said. "You ain't shot."

Instead of finding a pile of mangled flesh, all I saw was a spent fifty-caliber shell that had fallen from the sky as the Cobra passed over, and it had burned a brown spot on the back of his pant leg.

The firefight was over as quickly as it started, and we had escaped unscathed, except for a tiny burn on the back of one guy's leg. It had been a great and terrible day. Fear and anger gave way to giddy exhilaration as we made our way back to the LZ to await the birds that were bringing in a grunt company to sweep the area. The teammate with the legs that weren't shot off laughed harder than the rest of us when we told the story back at base. Life is grand when you think you're dead, but you discover you're alive.

The next day, we heard the full account of why the gunship fired without waiting for our smoke signal. The captain that we had met the day before, the commanding officer of the rapid response infantry company that replaced us on the ground, came to our Ranger barracks with a full explanation. It seems that a platoon of North Vietnamese soldiers, about thirty men, had unwittingly marched toward our *November Lima*, and the teammate that started shooting had merely seen the NVA point man bearing down on our position. When the firing started, the NVA panicked, unaware that there were only four of us. The Cobra didn't wait for our smoke

76

because the pilot saw the khaki clad men in pith helmets scattering across the grassy plain, and the Cobra miniguns mowed them down. Most, if not all, of the NVA platoon died that day.

My dad had served on a Navy Destroyer in the Pacific in WWII, a sleek and speedy escort that operated on the edge of the fleet, chasing Japanese subs and providing the first line of defense for air attacks. He told me of the excitement the crew felt one day when they pursued a Japanese submarine. They followed it on sonar back and forth, cat and mouse, and they dropped depth charges several times to no avail, as the thrill of the hunt heightened. Finally, when a smear of diesel fuel rose to the surface, the crew cheered their victory, as did my father. Only later did he feel the full impact of what had happened, of dead men in a sunk submarine, and he heaved his breakfast over the side of the ship.

I awoke the morning after our return lying in a puddle of my own puke on the concrete floor outside my bunk. An empty Jim Beam bottle stood silent vigil.

Donut Dollies

Mary took a pound of costly perfume made of pure nard, anointed Jesus' feet, and wiped them with her hair. The house was filled with the fragrance of the perfume.

John 12:3

We were celebrities.

The sideway glances at our tiger fatigues from the Remington Raiders and other warrior-wannabes who tramped the dusty roads of Camp Radcliffe said so. Maybe it was just a fashion thing. All the other swinging dicks at the sprawling base camp near An Khe wore standard-issue olive-drab fatigues and baseball caps, but the camo-clad Ranger lurps sported Australian cowboy hats with one side pinned up. You know, you just couldn't wear one of those without canting it sideways as if to say, yup, we're pretty hot shit.

Here's an example. We were on the chopper pad ready to be inserted on our latest mission. Half a dozen lurp teams were just a-smokin' and a-jokin' while we waited for the birds. When they arrived, they offloaded members of a good will tour from the states: NFL football players including Jack Snow, Floyd Little, Tucker Frederickson, and others. Of course, we were excited to see them and wanted pictures, but they were more interested in getting their pictures taken with the face-painted warriors in the tiger fatigues toting exotic weapons like an M-16 with a silencer, an M-16 over-under with an M-79 grenade launcher, and a few that weren't standard issue. We were unique, and we were celebrities.

But this is all background bullshit. This story is about the ladies who upstaged us. They were called "Donut Dollies."

A day or two before a mission, the lurp team leader and assistant would do a helicopter "fly-over" of the jungle domain that would become our God-forgotten Area of Operation for the next few days. We would identify primary and secondary landing zones and learn more about the terrain than our charts alone could tell us, but hard experience told us there were two worlds, the fantasy visible from the sky and the reality on the ground. The chopper view was a picture post card of steep mountain slopes of lush jungle and valleys carved by rivers stair cased with waterfalls. We knew the idyllic flyover would not reveal the snakes and tigers, much less the hooches of North Vietnamese way stations along the tributaries of the Ho Chi Minh trail that lay invisible under the triple canopy foliage, and that's why our sorry asses were needed to do recon in the bush.

I did it again. I digressed. Time to meet the dollies.

On one flyover, the chopper pilot said our return to base would be interrupted by an impromptu landing at a remote mountaintop firebase to pick up some extra passengers. I knew something was up

79

when the door gunners unfolded the seats attached to the back wall because we always plopped down right on the steel floor. Here's where I first met the donut dollies. Maybe it's racist of me to say that I was really, really tickled to see blonde, blue-eyed women again, but when four blushing dollies gingerly climbed aboard, assisted with the gentlemanly hand of the door gunner, the chronic foreboding that burned like an ulcer in my gut was momentarily forgotten.

There was little chance for small talk over the noise of the chopper blades, but during that ride back to base, our lurp celebrity status took a back seat to the honor accorded the feminine presence in short white dresses with Red Cross badges. The chopper pilot took us on a joyride, showing off—not for the lurps on board but for the dollies. Cresting a mountain range, the pilot dove his bird into a valley, gravity adding to the acceleration. Now the Huey helicopters we called slicks weren't real nimble, and they kind of lumbered along like airborne deuce-and-a-halfs, but the pilot that day put his bird through its paces. Like a nighthawk, the Huey abruptly flattened out its downward plunge just above the gurgling stream. For miles, the chopper curved along with the meandering blue line until it suddenly careened upward like a roller coaster in front of a wide but not too tall waterfall. Did I see NVA soldiers peering through the mist from a cave behind the falls, wondering at this exuberant display of airmanship?

Not that there weren't women around. There were Vietnamese washerwomen and other hooch-maids with passes into Camp Radcliffe to perform menial tasks. Some made money on the side (that is to say, on their backs), which recalls to mind the 18th birthday present for the farm boy from Kansas who had needed his parent's consent to join the army. He was a lurp in my platoon but not on my team. We paid for a whore to pop his cherry. He emerged from his mosquito-net covered bunk with a sheepish grin after just a minute or two, and the whore teased him because his pecker had squirted before he had penetrated.

Most of the time, the local city of An Khe was off limits, and we were confined to base, but a few teams were temporarily transferred to Ban Me Thuot a hundred miles south, and the local bar/night club, with prostitutes aplenty, became a daily attraction for some of my buddies. I only did it once, but I was uncomfortable. I knew she didn't get the twenty bucks, in military payment script, I plopped down, but the funds probably helped pay for a clip of bullets for the Russian AK-47 that would do me in. Her French features spoke to the unending war for her mother's people. The Ban Me Thuot bar scene was this shitty war in a nutshell.

Damn it, I did it again. Back to the dollies.

After I showered away the sweat, grime, and fear of the uneventful four day mission that followed our flyover, a couple of us headed for the Red Cross Rec Center where the smiling donut dollies dispensed cookies and Kool-Aid. We figured that sharing a helicopter ride had made us old friends. Like most of us, the dollies were here for a one-year tour. Unlike most of us, they were volunteers, but their plastered-on smiles barely veiled their aloofness. They were warned about the horny S.O.B.s who were thinking about their panties. It was like there was a sign on the door, "Look but don't touch."

That was part of it. But even more, it was don't get too close to the boy who might not return next week. Like the other females on the base, the nurses at the Camp Radcliffe hospital, the donut dollies saw wounds they couldn't heal, and the innocent idealism that brought them here had beaten a strategic retreat.

Like I said, we were celebrities according to our jaunty bush hats and tiger fatigues, and a couple of the dollies who had shared the chopper joyride actually stepped outside for a smoke with us, which seemed like a breach of Standard Operating Procedures. I think it was the Kansas connection. You see, in idle conversation it turns out that Peg, one of the dollies, hailed from a small Kansas town not fifty miles away from the homeland of the young farm boy who had tagged along that night. Spring breezes from Kansas, a world away, seemed to melt some of the ice. Hell, by the end of the night, we were all joking about Angus beef.

A week later, after another uneventful mission, I returned with the farm boy, who carried a special invitation to Peg, the dolly from

82

Kansas. Would the dollies care to come over to the Ranger compound for water buffalo steaks on the grill? I was surprised when they said yes, and a few days later Ranger jeeps unloaded half a dozen dollies from Kansas and other places that seemed to exist only in our distant memories to share beers and steaks. Under the circumstances, those tough water buffalo steaks were better than prime Angus. The dollies were friendlier in blue jeans and Bermuda shorts than in their sterile white duty dresses.

Over sizzling steaks on a grill, I caught the eye of Ann, with long, brown hair tied in a pair of pig-tails with furry red ribbons, and I offered her another beer, which she accepted, and we sat down around a makeshift picnic table and talked while dripping fat spattered onto hot coals. Ann had been on the helicopter joyride, but I hadn't seen her since that day. Straightaway, she made a show of her wedding band as if to warn that friendly conversation was all I should expect, and I was ok with that. Like the others, she was a college graduate, older than me, and I wondered at a married woman volunteering for the Nam, but I wasn't going to ask. Maybe it was just her way of keeping a distance. They say that your eyes are a window to your soul, but a smoky haze that said you can't come in clouded her gaze, and her narrow eye slits were out of place for what should have been round, brown and beautiful.

After we washed down our steaks with several beers, Ann dispensed with the small talk, and she cut right to the shit.

"Are you scared?"

"What, right now? Am I scared of you?" At first, I didn't catch her drift.

"No. I mean are you scared of dying? Are you scared when you go on a mission?"

What a dumb ass question. Of course we're scared when the chopper flies in low and we're hanging on, ready to jump into the tall grass, hoping there weren't any Charlies watching. Every uncertain step in the jungle was guided by fear of what we might step on or what noise we might make. Fear sat on my shoulder like the rat that climbed aboard one night while I pulled my two hour awake shift. Fear followed us back to our LZ and kicked us in the ass as we clambered aboard the birds that would carry us away.

I looked away and sucked deeply on my menthol cigarette. She said it, and now I was thinking it—no, more than that, I was feeling it—just like a fucking broad to ask "how does that make you feel?" I tried to be cool and blow smoke rings, but I coughed instead. Her simple question had poked like a punji stick, and my pent-up fears leaked out. I bit my lip, hard, and pretended that it was smoke that caused my eyes to well up. Like the crackling burst of an AK-47, deep-buried dread exploded all around. Sitting here, with a beer in one hand and a cig in the other, with a belly full of buffalo steaks, with a pig-tailed woman with smoky brown eyes scouring my soul

84

laid-bare, the hope of home was drowned out by wave after wave of anguish. I was here, and home was there.

Ann glanced at the others and tugged at my sleeve.

"Let's walk." She saved me from embarrassment, and we moved onto a nearby knoll and watched the stars until we heard the jeep engines fire up, and then she was gone with Peg and the others.

Two weeks later, I returned the favor. When I arrived in the barracks following a mission, there was an urgent message from Ann, and I went straightaway to the Rec Center before I even cleaned up.

"I can't talk now," she said. The protective glaze over her eyes seemed thinner, and darkness seeped through. "Come to the women's quarters around seven this evening."

The women at Camp Radcliffe, the dollies and the nurses, had their own compound in the center of the base. Ringed with concertina wire and sand bags, the place had the look of a prison, and a pair of GIs with sidearms and M-16s guarded the only entrance, but they weren't there to keep the women in but the men out. I wasn't sure what to do, but when I explained why I was there, they rang up on a landline, and soon Ann appeared and ushered me inside. She shared a cramped room with a nurse who was on duty at the hospital, so we were alone. There were two pictures on a small night stand next to the head of her bunk: Ann in a wedding dress with her husband on their wedding day and a picture of him alone in an Army Class A uniform with a purple heart draped over the picture frame. There was also a half-full bottle of Cutty Sark and an empty glass.

She sat on her bunk, and I sat across on the nurse's bunk. Conversation was choppy until she blurted it out.

"He's dead," she said. "Our farm boy's dead, and his body is in a bag on its way to Kansas."

Nobody told me, and I hadn't heard. I was too quick to shower and head on over here. I hadn't even eaten in the mess hall, but now my empty stomach jumped, and I might have retched if there had been anything to heave. Ann lit a cigarette and passed it to me. She poured a couple of fingers of scotch into the empty glass and handed that to me also. My hands were shaking.

"Peg is in a rage, and she's taking it on herself," Ann said. "Peg wailed over and over again that she should have made love to him when they had the chance."

Ann took a deep breath then exhaled slowly. She leaned back with her arms bracing on the bunk and stared at the ceiling. Without emotion, she repeated Peg's words. "He asked me to, said he'd never done it before, not really, and he wanted to do it with me for his first time, but dollies don't do that, and now he's dead. I should have done it. I should have done that much. I should have made love to him, his first and his last," and then Ann lost it, and she sobbed. I wanted to reach out, to touch her, to hold her, but …

After a few moments, all was silent save the strains of Blood, Sweat and Tears that seeped in from a nearby hooch … *there'll be one child born in this world to carry on, to carry on* … Ann wasn't sobbing anymore, just sniffling, and she blew her runny nose into a tissue. And then she looked up at me, and her round, brown eyes were the size of the moon. She peeled off her olive-drab T shirt up and over her head, and she wasn't wearing a bra.

"Hold me," she said. "Hold me close, and make love to me until the sun comes up," and I did.

Down by the Riverside

Gonna lay down my sword and shield
Down by the riverside
Down by the riverside
Down by the riverside
Gonna lay down my sword and shield
Down by the riverside

Verse from *Down by the Riverside,* a traditional gospel song.

As the first slivers of dawn filtered through the mist rising from the river, I nervously fidgeted with the thumb trigger of a fifty caliber machine gun atop a Patton tank. I was a newbie, a fucking new guy, and my first excursion outside a base camp was to pull overnight guard duty from the turret of a tank that guarded a bridge over a river. The river flowed through a village just outside the base camp. As the gray dawn arrived, I heard the first stirrings of life, and ghostly shapes floated in the mist. How the hell was I supposed to know who was friendly and who was enemy? I figured I wouldn't know until someone blew my head off or slid a satchel charge under the tank. When the sun peaked over the mountains, the shapes materialized, and I realized that the villagers had merely assembled to await the opening of the bridge. When a jeep pulled up to take me back to base, I breathed again.

Much later, when I was a lurp, there was one advantage to pulling recon missions deep in the jungle. We always operated in a "free-fire" zone, and we didn't have to wonder. The Vietnamese we encountered were NVA regulars, and there was no ambiguity. In a free-fire zone, all the villagers and farmers--fathers, mothers, children, grandparents and grandkids--had been forcibly removed and relocated and warned against return. "If you stay there, you're liable to get shot." Or bombed. Or doused with Agent Orange. By definition, anyone present in a free-fire zone was deemed to be the enemy. For lurp teams, every mission was into a free-fire zone, and we were free to fire at anything or anyone because there weren't any friendlies there.

Or, so we were told.

On the mission when we lost our naiveté, we had been inserted onto a plain dotted with clumps of bushy trees surrounded by tall elephant grass, and we immediately stumbled across signs of habitation that made us wonder about the presence of women and children.

"What's up?" we asked base through our PRC-25 radio. "Is our intelligence skewed? There appear to be non-combatants present in our AO."

"Wait one," base replied, but then the response came quickly. "Our policy is to shoot first and ask questions later. It's a free-fire zone, and the four of you can't risk asking, 'are you friend or foe?'"

The higher-ups back in the rear issued the policy, but the onus was on us--four scared young men--to carry it out. "Shoot first," they said.

Sure enough, later that day, we heard the laughter of approaching women and giggles of children. "Shit," I mumbled as we hunkered down in the tall grass. We hoped they would pass by, unaware of our watchful eyes and nervous trigger fingers, but they only came closer. "Go away," I silently mouthed the words. "Turn around."

They didn't; they headed straight toward us. Closer and closer they came until we could see the conical bamboo hats of the women and could hear the crunch of the grass under their feet. Another few paces, and they would step on us.

That's when we did it. That's when we jumped up. That's when we disobeyed orders.

"Get the hell out of here," we shouted as we flailed our arms. Like squawking hens, the women led their shrieking children away.

One remained. An old woman with a face wrinkled like a raisin simply stared. After a brief hesitation, she raised a bony finger. First, she tugged at the silk strap beneath her chin that held her hat in place, then she raised the crooked finger to her lips--did she *shush* us?--and then she tugged at the brim of her hat, pulling it low over her eyes. With a faint smile lifting the corners of her mouth, she raised her head to take a last look at us before slowly turning and following the others. We beat a quick retreat in the opposite direction.

So far, I've just been providing backstory and prologue. Time now to tell you about the mission down by the riverside that would be our last mission together, the four young men of Romeo 18.

****

Sometimes the LZ was hot, sometimes it was thick with punji sticks like the quills on a porcupine's back, sometimes it was a postage stamp opening amongst tall trees, sometimes it hung along a steep mountain slope, but this one was as easy as landing on a golf course back home. Our chopper damn near landed, which allowed us to step off rather than jump. The LZ was wide and flat with short tufts of what looked like Bermuda grass instead of head-high elephant grass. During our approach, the choppers swooped over a gurgling stream--shallow with huge gray rocks and sand bars creating eddies in the swift current--that formed the eastern edge of the LZ, and it looked to be a grove of banana trees at the far west end. Two slicks came in one right after the other, each loaded with four sorry-assed lurps. The other chopper offloaded first, and the team scrambled into the bush to the north. Our chopper followed right behind, but we hustled into the tree line on the south side of the LZ. For the next four or five days, they would hole up in the jungle on that side, and we would ascend the ridge that commanded a view of the river on our side.

After we entered the tangle of brush under teak and wild rubber trees, we slowed to our jungle walk, step-by-slow-step, eyes darting back and forth, ears straining and filtering all sounds, and we started to ease our way to the top of the ridgeline that overlooked the river. The chirping birds and chattering rodents said all was well, but then without warning we were knocked flat on our asses from the concussion of one helluva explosion. Flying sticks and other crud pelted us, and we hunkered down.

"What the fuck!"

Charlie didn't have anything like what just hit us. My ears were ringing from the explosion, but I heard the team leader bellow on his radio.

"Base, base, this is Romeo 18, come in, come in for chrissake,"

"Go ahead Romeo 18. This is base." I heard the exchange on my own radio.

"Some assholes are shootin' at us, and it ain't Charlie. It could be artillery, but it seems too big. Must be the Air Force. Get those motherfuckers off our back!"

A minute passed, then two, then ten. No more explosions, and then a new voice squeaked on the radio. It was the pilot on a spotter plane for the jets that dropped bombs and fired missiles.

"This is bird dog on your push. Sorry, Romeo 18, we didn't know you were there. Hope you're all ok. At least, you have a story to tell your grandkids."

Fucking asshole. I had more than enough stories to tell the grandkids that I probably wasn't going to have anyhow. Fucking free-fire zone. The good news was that any Charlies in that vicinity must be shitting their shorts and hauling ass back towards Hanoi.

We moved more quickly than normal to the ridgeline, and we settled into a thick stand of bamboo. We didn't have much of a view of the river below--too damned much brush--but we could see one small patch where the current split around a gray chunk of rock smack dab in the center of the river. As we boiled water over a lump of C-4 plastic explosive for our freeze-dried LRRP rations, the melody of the gurgling stream soothed our frayed nerves as pale-yellow dusk seeped into the forest. During the last hour of daylight, a cacophony of croaking frogs drowned out the sounds of running water. As night fell, a bright-orange moon lifted over the ridgeline across the river.

I was due for the fourth and final two-hour watch, so I wrapped myself in my poncho liner and soon was dreaming of catching smallmouth bass in a Canadian stream. Just a few springs earlier, my dad took my younger brother and me on a Canadian fishing trip to celebrate my graduation from high school. We trudged through the Canadian forest following a fast flowing stream, and we caught chunky bronze backs with every cast of our frog-tipped hooks into eddies behind the rocks, and then my dream returned me to the front yard of the house I grew up in and Dad was shaking my hand, hard, and I saw mist in his eyes for the first time ever as we said our goodbyes before I was off to the airplane that would carry me to Fort Lewis and then onto Vietnam. I awoke and listened for the frogs, but they had quieted so I watched wispy clouds drift across the moon face for a while before sleep again claimed me.

After that frisky first day, our mission settled into four days of solitude, interrupted by the radio voices of the nearby team on the other side of the meadow. We heard their conversations with base, and we added a little smart talk of our own.

"A gook just walked by us," the radio crackled, and we listened closely as our own sense of alert spiked.

"Next time, grab him," came the response from base. "Remember, teams get an in-country three-day R&R for capturing a POW." Since the primary purpose of lurp teams was recon and intelligence gathering, it made sense that a captured NVA soldier would be a plum source of valuable information about activity in that AO, more than we could learn by simply watching the river flow by.

94

That's when we started blathering with the other team about snatching a prisoner and the good times we would have in Vung Tau, a city on the seacoast near Saigon--three days of beaches, booze, and babes. Every swinging dick in Vietnam would get one week of R&R out of country in places like Australia, Bangkok, and Hong Kong--or Hawaii for the married dudes--but an in-country three day R&R in Vung Tau was a rare incentive prize.

The POW conversation lasted the rest of the afternoon, but the next few days passed uneventfully, and there were no more enemy sightings, and the smart talk about catching a POW was merely that.

Until we returned to the LZ.

On the day of extraction, it was SOP to move to the LZ an hour or two before the birds were expected. That would allow plenty of time to get there without rushing, to allow the forest to settle down after we moved through, and to allow us to scope out any signs of enemy activity around the LZ. We departed the safety of the bamboo thicket and slowly worked our way down to the LZ and settled into a corner of the rain forest on the riverbank that overlooked a broad expanse of river directly in front of us. We were immediately adjacent to the wide open spaces of the LZ on our left flank--a perfect vantage point to watch and wait.

It was then that base reported that our extraction birds had been diverted, and we wouldn't be coming out that day.

95

"Shit."

We had three piss-poor options. We could head back to our comfortable hidey-hole in the bamboo thicket atop the ridge, we could search out another *November Lima* nearby, or we could spend the night right there, down by the riverside. There was thin brush around us, but not as thick as the bamboo shoots atop the ridge. Based on the slant of the sun that was setting over the banana grove to the west, it seemed to make the most sense to leave our sorry asses right where we sat even if we were more exposed than we would like. Darkness would be upon us soon enough. We ate a hasty, uncooked meal, and I dozed off while leaning against my ruck, but my eyes blinked wide open when a hand covered my mouth to keep me quiet. It was the team leader, and he jerked his head toward the river.

On the opposite side, about fifty meters away, a man stood knee deep in the flowage, right at river's edge. He occasionally leaned over and doused his hands in the current. Was he washing himself? Was he washing dishes? Washing clothes? He wore only shorts or a loin cloth, not the khaki fatigues or pith helmet of the NVA. His shock of unkempt black hair was tinged with gray. Did he have a weapon lying on the bank?

Suddenly, he was gone. He had disappeared as silently and mysteriously as he had appeared. *Whew*. We collectively exhaled and looked at each other with puzzled expressions. "Who was that?

What was that all about? Was that the cook for an NVA camp on the other side?"

I didn't doze off again, and we were all wide awake as two younger men soon materialized in the same spot across the river, but they didn't remain stationary. They also wore short pants plus loose fitting shirts, and they carried woven baskets as they crossed the river, unaware of our wide eyes like a cat watching a mouse. They didn't appear to be carrying any weapons, but who knew what might be tucked away in the folds of their baggy shirts. They seemed completely at ease as they climbed the river bank about fifteen meters in front of the muzzles of our M-16s that followed their every step. They disappeared across the broad meadow of the LZ in the direction of the banana grove on the far end.

"We should grab one of those sons-of-bitches."

POW talk bubbled up again, and base encouraged us; we quickly hatched a plan and a backup: plan A and plan B.

Plan A: If and when another Charlie would cross the river, we would wait until he was fully exposed and vulnerable in the middle of the stream. That's when we would spring our trap. First step, I would fire a warning shot that would splash water near the man. Second step, we would stand up and point our weapons at him. Third step, we would all holler *dung lai,* which we understood to mean "stop." Fourth step, our prisoner would throw up his hands and surrender, and we'd be on our way to Vung Tau.

97

Plan B: If the man didn't immediately surrender, I would fire a second shot, this time aiming at his legs to disable him. He would then be forced to surrender.

We were ready, and soon one of the young men who had passed in front of us returned and began to cross back over the river. He now balanced his basket on his head--one hand held it steady. I waited until he was midstream, as we planned. I fired a warning shot, as we planned. We all hollered, as we planned, but the son-of-a-bitch didn't *dung lai,* as planned; instead, he took one look in our direction and began to run, as best he could in knee-deep water, toward the other side. I put plan B into effect and fired a second shot at his legs, but he kept running.

"Shit," I said as I lowered my rifle to my side. We had no plan C.

I wasn't expecting what happened next. The two young guys on our team, eighteen and nineteen years old, each emptied a full clip of their M-16s at the fleeing man. When I looked back at the river, his body was sprawled across a sand bar, and his basket bobbed its way downstream. Our plans had gone horribly wrong.

Our team leader was immediately on the horn reporting the contact to base.

"Check the body for documents," came the response.

What the fuck. We'd be shot to pieces if anybody watched from the other side.

"There's no cover," the team leader said on the radio. "The body's lying right in the middle of the friggin' river. It's nuts to wade out there to check for documents that probably ain't there, anyway."

Nonsense was spiraling out of control. Base was insistent, and there was an implied warning that we needed to bring back proof that we had actually checked the body. We didn't think it through, and we didn't figure a way to fake it, so we went; the team leader and I splashed out there against our better judgment as quickly as we could. We ripped the bloody shirt off the dead man for our proof, rolled him over, and stripped off his wristwatch for good measure. Of course, there were no documents and no weapon. He was just a fucking teenager, probably younger than the two men who had gunned him down and now covered us from the riverbank. I purposely checked the back of his legs, and there was a small puncture wound and a dab of blood where my bullet had entered, but it hadn't stopped him. Probably missed his femur by less than an inch. *Jesus fucking Christ.* We rushed back and scrambled up the riverbank.

****

99

Hours later in the dark hours of the night, the team leader and I sat in our barracks and worked to kill a fifth of bourbon. We had showered off the sweat, grime, and face paint, but we couldn't scrub deep enough. We puzzled over and over again why fate had brought us together with those three guys in the bush. Who were they? What were they doing there? We tried really hard to convince ourselves that they were NVA, but we feared they were just a grandpa and his two grandsons who had refused to leave the jungle. Probably Montagnards. Fucking free-fire zone. Fucking shoot first and ask questions later. Fucking three day R&R.

And then we did what we often did. The team leader pulled out his guitar, and we sang through a repertoire that included songs of Pete Seeger; Peter, Paul, and Mary; and the Kingston Trio. We had stepped outside to let others in the barracks sleep, and we serenaded the sunrise with an old gospel classic, "Down by the Riverside."

> Gonna stick my sword in the golden sand;
> Down By the riverside
> Down by the riverside
> Down by the riverside
> Gonna stick my sword in the golden sand
> Down by the riverside
> Gonna study war no more.

By the time we had repeated the refrain after each verse, six or seven times, our mind was made up.

> I ain't gonna study war no more,

100

I ain't gonna study war no more,
Study war no more.
I ain't gonna study war no more,
I ain't gonna study war no more,
Study war no more.

Right after breakfast in the mess hall, the team leader and I showed up at company headquarters where we had been debriefed the night before. We wanted out, though we didn't quite put it that way. The team leader requested a transfer to a rear echelon unit for the duration of his tour. To our surprise, the first sergeant showed more empathy than we expected and granted his request. I reminded the sergeant that I was a short-timer with little time remaining before my tour was up. According to informal company policy, short-timers didn't pull missions to the field, and I spent my last days and weeks in Vietnam hanging out and getting high.

I wore that boy's wristwatch until it stopped--not as war booty but as a sign of penance that only I understood. Whenever I checked the time, I wished I could turn the hours backward.

About the Author

Obie Holmen was born and raised in central Minnesota. After graduating from Dartmouth College and serving with the US Army in Viet Nam as a LRRP (scout), he returned to Minnesota to study at the University of Minnesota Law School. He was a trial attorney in St. Cloud, Minnesota, for a quarter century. He is the author of a work of historical fiction, *A Wretched Man, a novel of Paul the apostle*, that was released to critical acclaim and an enthusiastic readership in 2010, and in 2014 Pilgrim Press released his non-fiction, historical account of the gay and lesbian journey to full inclusion in their church entitled, *Queer Clergy: A History of Gay and Lesbian Ministry in American Protestantism.*

The author refers to this novella as "autobiographical fiction." True incidents serve as inspiration for each chapter, but the stories are told with literary embellishment. An early reviewer suggests the writing is *bold, dark, and intense*, and that is an apt characterization of the Vietnam experience. The photo above is the author when he served with K Company, 75th Infantry (Rangers) in the central highlands of Vietnam in 1969-70. During his tour of duty, he was twice awarded a bronze star for valor in combat.

Each of the individual chapters are available separately, or the entire book may be purchased as an eBook or print paperback. *Eleven Bravo* introduces a newbie grunt infantryman arriving in Vietnam, and *Humping* recounts a torturous twenty-three day trek through the jungle for the newbie's infantry company. *Here Comes Charlie* introduces the LRRP reconnaissance team, beginning with a helicopter insertion and ending with an encounter with North

103

Vietnamese regulars--the NVA. *Whiskey in the Rain* is a series of vignettes recounting alcohol and drug use. *Cat Quiet* stealth is their only ally as the four Lurps creep through the jungle with striped face paint and tiger fatigues. *Chasing After Wind* considers twists of fate in the context of a barracks poker game, the uncontrollable wind, and a malevolent joker in the deck. Calling down fire upon enemies, like Elijah in the Old Testament, is the theme of *Elijah Fire*. There were women in Vietnam, nurses and *Donut Dollies*--Red Cross volunteers who bolstered troop morale. *Down by the Riverside* concludes the book, and the old gospel spiritual by that name serves as inspiration for the chapter and one stanza provides the book title, *Gonna Stick my Sword in the Golden Sand*.

For more information about the author and his writing, see www.rwholmen.com.

Made in the USA
Coppell, TX
05 July 2020